SEMIOTEXT(E) NATIVE AGENTS SERIES

Published by Semiotext(e)
2007 Wilshire Blvd., Suite 427, Los Angeles, CA 90057
www.semiotexte.com

The author wishes to thank Brian Tennessee Claflin and Mario Dzurila.

Cover art and Frontpiece by Bjarne Melgaard, *Untitled*, 2011. Pencil on paper, 36 x 28 cm (14 x 11 inches). Courtesy Rod Bianco Gallery, Oslo.

Back Cover Photography by Nicola Guiducci
Design by Hedi El Kholti

ISBN: 978-1-58435-125-2
Distributed by The MIT Press, Cambridge, Mass. and London, England
Printed in the United States of America

THE SUICIDERS

Travis Jeppesen

\<e\>

for J.C., C.B.C., N.S.

Wer rastet, der rostet.
— German idiom

CHAPTER 1

The friends. The house. A spider, a dwarf, a parrot, and some names.

The house, a Gothic approximation of a dump with lots of stains, abandoned when found. Matthew's friends were there a lot—when they weren't running away. To keep him company, he bought himself a fat fuck parrot. Fed it dead possum every night at the same hour—when he remembered he was still alive. The parrot's name was Jesus H. Christ. Matthew sat there. Adam is over on the floor. Peter sniffing whiteout. Yellow cup drools. I have so many friends.

The friends had stopped going to school. They had better things to do, like fuck knows what. They would be great artists some day, if only you could learn to consider death an art. Get that fucking whiteout out of your nose, Peter. The whiteout is my muse, Peter responds. A milk stain around his nostrils. God-damn entropy hovering like a cloud.

Peter disarranged some wires. Some fancy music got played. A song of evil spirits getting naked in the zoo. Let's go to the zoo! Matthew protested. Which one am I. I don't want to go to the zoo, they don't have any goddamn art there. Matthew will be a pedophile and look at all the children. Children have brains they don't get for free. Their parents must pay a lot of money for them. Then they destroy the state, everyone gets fucked in the ass. My sooty membranous gyration.

I decided to go take a dump and read the bible. Multi-tasking has come to define this century I woke up one day and found myself in. You can't blame us for the state of the world. We're just some teenage kids with bad hair.

Adam, meanwhile, was squeaking. One of the reasons he got kicked out of school. Because he'd just sit there all day making high-pitched noises to himself. Like a mouse dying of cancer but really really enjoying it.

Pretty song plays. Adam bit himself just for fun. Bit his wrist until the blood came. Flowers for Algernon. That's the name of the TV Movie of the Week. Forcefeed television demented fears, it will reciprocate via Evening News. Jesus H. Christ flew over, landed on Adam's head, fluttered its feathers. Hey Matthew, can a parrot fart?

Adam continued to squeak. Matthew picked up a guitar. Peter covered himself with a blanket. He wanted to forget something. He didn't remember what.

Joy can only be excavated from ruins. It has to match a definition of primal. Every which way you yearn, you still prefer doing nothing. Maybe that's what's so philosophical about your bodily movements.

I want to go to the zoo. I want to go to the zoo. I want to go to the zoo. I want to go.

The teenagers had so many friends. That's why they didn't need each other—they had all the others. Still, they wanted. One day you will grow up and want something too, then you'll realize it's all been a big mistake. I cleaned my butthole with a page of genesis. I found the story dry. Whoever wrote the bible didn't understand the mechanics of language. Not the way Adam does. He's a real poet, sitting over there squeaking. Sometimes when he gets carried away, little white yeast balls appear in the corners of his mouth. The teacher threw him out of class. Then he came over here where he could squeak in peace, away from the dictates of the western world. Here, we leave our televisions on in silence. You can even make love to the radiator if you want. Situational broadcast from the radio in the kitchen. Sometimes I go in there to hallucinate a girl. She never comes back twice. She must be afraid of what she finds.

The house we found ourselves. Didn't even cost nothing. People moved out, no one wanted it, we invented ourselves in here. Rush through the introductions so as to not find out too much about each other. The only thing we had in common was this desire to be teens for the rest of our circumstance.

Satan's ashtray. This part of the world the sun don't come out too often. At least we had the animals. The animals are there for us when the sun isn't. Sometimes you dream the animals going into the sun. The sun swallows all the animals on this planet and burns them up into magma. We have to live in a world without animals, it is so sad, you want to die. But you become an animal instead, and therefore death will never come to you. Peter bit himself again. Or was it Matthew this time. Wait I'm so confused. I have difficulty telling my friends apart from one another. That is because they all look exactly the same. The same stringy black hair, empty eye sockets, hollowed-out expression. My friends are merely effigies I keep to remind me of the animal inside my mind.

A cherry-flavored tiger one for breakfast. Apricot pussy for dessert. A corpse called your mother. Are you going to school tomorrow? Laugh at the funny joke guys. He'll never go back to school again. Not after this disaster area. Watchfulness; you have to keep aware, the authorities. The satellite expression. Adam stood up, walked across the room. His head drooped to accommodate his maudlinity. He tripped over a shoe, but then it turned out to be not a shoe at all, only the shadow of a shoe. I think I sprained my ankle. Then he drank a gallon of spoilt milk.

Our bass player just died of heavy metal music. The music told him where to go and he followed. It was so sad, all our friends came to the funeral. They wanted to pay their respects to something they'd never have the language to understand. Once they all realized how dumb they were, they started laughing right over his grave. Heavy metal music played, and all my friends fell in. The bulldozer came and now I don't have to deal with that particular shade of reality no more.

He mutilated the half-tone conversation with his wand. Adam half wanted to become a wizard ever since he saw that movie, but none of the tricks he tried out worked for him. That's one of the reasons why he started cutting himself, I suppose. He stares at a picture of himself on the wall. He squeaks to himself in a made-up language. This language is so private, I'm not allowed to reproduce it here. You will just have to move in with us if you want to learn something.

Oh all my endeavors. They have left me with a ringing in my ears. I took my foot to the dentist to get it fixed. He removed all three of Matthew's teeth. That is more than any of us deserve. I sniffed some more. Pink dots appear on the ceiling. If only I weren't so against it. My thing is to make the silence an outfit I can wear when I go to my favorite shopping mall. Flowerpot falls out of the window, lands on our neighbor's head down below. Sorry, whatever your name is. I'm thinking about fire this week also.

Blood is one way to isolate yourself; words are another. Adam sits down on top of my imaginary friend. Get off him you pervert. I don't want to have an honest discussion right now, okay? There are gramophones that will fit up your ass. Matthew in the kitchen trying to make a cup out of sugar. Can we steal more furniture, guys. Go into the forest and fashion a couch with the twigs you find there. I'm afraid of the forest at nighttime. But it's two o'clock in the afternoon, dingus. It's still dark, though. That's because you forgot to cut your hair.

Winter tends to last a long time. A cat in the windowsill. Matthew sits on Adam's face. Farts out a volcano. Let's take a roadtrip, you guys—still sitting there. Adam doesn't seem to mind. Maybe that's because he has no mind. He's so burnt out on substance, he's not even real no more. He's just a living breathing body with no reality to call his own. I think you're straight, he says. No, he's a fag. Maybe he's bisexual. Maybe he's trisexual. Maybe he's a transvestite. Maybe he's transgendered. Maybe he's a hermaphroditic dwarf with no future. Maybe his genitals can't be transfigured into a name. Go away, you anus.

Anus McGuinness is a name Peter calls Matthew at times. But we have all sorts of names for one another. Sometimes Matthew is Marc. At other times Peter is Marc. Then there are times when Adam is Steven. Mostly, though, we prefer Lukas. Lukas for Matthew and Peter, of course. Lukas could never be Adam. Adam is more like an invocation for Marc. Marc being the persona created by Peter. Peter isn't his real name anyway. His real name is Samson. But even before he was Samson, he was really Peter. Except for that phase when he was Andrew. But he never likes to talk about that period, it was really rough for all of us. In those days Adam was Marc. Matthew got upset, stole that name away from him. I almost became Peter the other night, but decided to remain Zach. At times I squeak just like Adam, but I remain Zach. A name is a core. I can only respond to whispers.

Who threw out those goddamn boxes I needed those for my dead canary collection, shouts Peter, Peter coming into the room screaming at everyone like his goddamn dick got stuck in an electrical socket. Hey Peter, you can't talk to us like that, said Adam, we are supposed to be your friends. If you were my friend, you wouldn't have thrown out all the boxes. Now it's raining and the boxes have melted into the cement outside. Wanna see for yourself? No, I don't like looking. Well, I can't blame you, but next time, could you please do me a favor and ask before you throw out anything. What about a chicken wing? Can I throw one of those out sometime? Sure, just take a photo of it before you do. That's all I ask of you. Samson.

Diarrhea in your brain. Call out nuclear holocaust to the late arrivals. We are spending one more week at the end of time. After that it all becomes over. *Over* in big fat capital letters. Here, tell me a quick story about the endgame.

You hear a knife being sharpened in the kitchen; you look outside and see a raven. See, even transsexuals have names.

It's so desperate, to have an illusion all over the floor. My life is a toilet of recycled objects. I remember entire days of not moving, staying completely still, just to see what would happen. Muscles atrophy, the toenails fall off one by one. You collect them all in a soup can and take them down to the salvation army to make a donation. They don't want it, so you're sent back home, a milkman once again. Nothing to do but put the toenails in the frying pan, summon a shaman.

It is important to go away from here at times, I know this now. Hey guys, should we take a little vacation? I don't know how, I have no money. We can steal our parents' car and depart this world for one last time, if you know what I'm truly saying. I'd rather sniff whiteout and fake death, says Peter. You don't know what you're saying, Adam. Of course I don't—that's precisely why I said it. People only say things they don't know, can't understand. That's what social discourse means. The words when spoken collide into each other, and in that explosion, meaning gets formed. Some spend their lives chasing after it, never really understanding the process until it's too late. Once that happens, they're already trapped in a delusion bubble. That bubble pops, and little babies float up to the ceiling.

We've had up halloween decorations from over a year ago. No those cobwebs are real. Why don't we take them down. I can't answer such formulations, there's no question mark at the end. Outside, a small dog barks into a microphone; New Orleans. That wasn't a place you escaped from until a few years ago. A kidnapped child is better than not having a childhood.

Suicide satellite burns up the shadow at times. Salvation screaming out the window. Jesus H. just flew away.

The coffee sweats when you cook it. Chinese noodles for breakfast again. Sometimes we talk about hiring a young girl to come clean up after us. I'm sorry did I just step on your foot. Okay then I'm glad I didn't.

Adam slides the tape into the VCR. It's our favorite movie, I have to admit. Sometimes life gets stained with a collection of rotten memories. Like the one I'm having now. A cow just fell out of the window.

My mother always told me to be wary of anyone bold enough to assert who they are. I guess that's why people like to relax in front of me. Are you regular? An image flickers on the screen. Dwarf bukkake party. One teenage dwarf has no skin. She rubs her tiger breasts in front of the hung young Latino with the sour expression on his mouth. He doesn't want to taste any flavors that can't be store-bought. An anorexic legacy of terminal illusions. He will put his penis inside just to satisfy her. Another dwarf is male. He has to fuck a fully grown woman. I think we like to watch the dwarves fuck because it gives us a reason to live. At least that's what Matthew said once. Can you believe him? I can't. He just stepped on my mother's foot. I didn't even know your mother was over here. She came to pick up the stains from last night. Give your face a window to look out of. A lamplight on the other. Greed is my salvation; the dwarf just ejaculated on another midget's face.

Adam takes out his boner, starts headbanging with devil horns raised high in the air. A representative of this delusion. Dream forecast keeps you wide awake. One of the dwarves comes out of the TV screen, crawls into the living room. Comes face-to-face with Adam's boner. Adam's boner has a face on it, you see. Dwarf proceeds to lick that face.

Don't fuck the dwarf without us, you traitor. We're the Suiciders. Everything we do we do together until the day comes when our animals will eat us. Say bye to your mother, we're watching porn.

Didn't Lukas tell you? Adam's mother did porn too. Shut up, fuckface. There is no benevolence. There is only the juice of freedom. Drink it till you puke. Just don't get any on the TV screen. Not while I'm masturbating.

The feeling is constant: no relief.

Spiders crawl out of the dwarf's butthole. Adam is surprised. He catches one of them, says he wants to keep it as a pet. The only rule is he's not allowed to give it a name.

I take a photograph in order to cherish this moment forever. I don't want to see it go. But I know I've already stuck my thing inside the dwarf; soon it will all be over. The word *over* in capital letters. The dwarf shrieks as it chokes on Adam's boner. A pornographic whirlwind. I wish we had a camera here to cherish this moment forever. Instead we will have to keep it inside ourselves; memory can't be trusted. Memory is a pathological liar without a state. You can't call the police on memory, you can only use a stick to banish it.

Whenever I hear someone screaming, I think about freedom. The dwarf's head just crashed through the television screen. Now you ruined the image forever, Matthew shrieked. I was just getting ready to ejaculate all over this pretty lampshade, too. Stop sulking, Matthew. You can always call Adam's mother over here. Shut up, fuckface. Adam don't hit me, you know I'm allergic to violence.

Let's invite a bunch of children over and encourage them to talk about memory why don't we I want to see what they'll have to say. Making love to the radiator is so much fun. Dead dwarf don't like no bukkake. There Adam, your spider is trying to escape back into the realm of buttholeland. Don't let him. I will make a leash out of string so that I can walk him around the neighborhood. You can't go outdoors here Adam this place is dangerous. There are cops and homeless people all around. We were homeless once too before we found this place. We don't want to get found out, or else it's back to school for all of us once again. School—yuck. I don't want to learn about slavery.

Should we give the dwarf a name? Not the dwarf, just its corpse. That would resolve things. Yeah, you're right, I hate it when that happens. We'll go into the kitchen, build him a coffin out of sugar. That way the decomposition process won't take so goddamn long.

Adam's pet spider crawled up his left nostril to take a nap. Matthew made coffee. Peter has so many friends, you just wouldn't believe. So many of us died that year; we had bad luck. But then another year would come to make us all alive again.

We sat up all night playing bored games and fantasizing bloody murder. Adam doesn't have school in the morning. Good. He can make us all toast. Look—out the window—our dwarf chasing after a rabbit. Guess he's not so dead after all. But soon, the rabbit will be.

CHAPTER 2

The friends decide to go on a journey to the
end of the world.
They meet a **Whore** along the way
and become **Suiciders.**
They can't find Jesus!

L ukas (this was Peter's name again all of a sudden) got his GF preggers so they went out to find an abortionist to take it away from them and put it in a trash can where it belongs. They left Adam at home with his creepy butthole spider, me and all my friends staring at the ceiling fan, wishing we had a midget to define us. Zach came up with a wonderful idea: Let's kill ourselves. Great, I suggested, but first, let's take the world out with us. How do we do that, began Adam, whose spider hung in the shape of a question mark from his knee, I mean, we do not even have a high school education.

Here comes the retard from next door. She's always coming over here looking for Matthew. She has a real thing for him, I don't know why. After all we've put her through. There was the time we took her out to the woods, stuck a dead squirrel up her pussy. We told her we'd give her five bucks if she did it, then we took a picture and ran away. Adam used to have it as the screen saver on his computer, before his computer died. Now that's an image that will just have to remain burned into the sides of our brains. So that we can laugh to ourselves for no apparent reason whenever she stalks by.

Adam's running around squeaking like a mouse. He can't control the voices in his head and he doesn't want to. His version of freedom makes me so horny. We got into a car and drove to the other continent; we had to pick Lukas up from the abortion clinic. Did they let you watch the proceedings? When they took it out of her, it looked like the inside of a jelly doughnut. It made me hungry. Can we stop up here at the Donut Hole?

In an ideal world, we would all be retarded. That's why they invented drugs, to get rid of all the burdens. Before we went to the other continent, we had a few pitstops to make. Wait, are all my friends here? I just have to make sure. I can't travel anywhere without them. No reason to download any new ones. My first friend was Adam. We met in art class. I liked him because there was nothing to understand. That made it easy to be myself (someone else). Dry rot invades the ceiling. We had to get out of the house that was holding us prisoner. Another continent is never far away.

It's not because he did acid, it's because of the voices, the squeaky voices—that's why Adam got kicked out, Lukas protests. Don't contradict me, I said. We're all dropouts because we see the future. Lukas what's that on your t-shirt.

Lukas left school too. One day all the kids made fun of him. It's because he overslept, just grabbed the first t-shirt he could find, laying next to his bed. The t-shirt turned out to be a cum rag. The other kids saw the splatterments and laughed. He was so embarrassed, he set the school on fire and ran away.

Matthew has a third testicle. Adam has a pet spider. Lukas

has so many friends. I want to go to the zoo. We will invade something instead.

I just stared at the illusion. You're supposed to be driving the car, doofus. To fuck is to be free on top of someone.

Hey guys, did you remember to bury that dwarf? Oh fuck we had better go back to the house then. No, don't you remember, the wolves came and ate him? In his coffin made of sugar. Oh I feel bad for the wolves then, they must have diabetes now. No, that's taken care of, I called the dialectician and reported it. He came and captured the wolves and now they're undergoing insulin treatment. Black wolf died but you won't go to jail. You can't go to jail in this country for accidentally making a black wolf eat a sugar midget corpse.

They were on a mission. A mission to recover Jesus H. Christ, who had flown away from them. They weren't feeding her enough meat, so she got mad and went away. When you have a pet parrot, you really should feed it with the brains of smaller animals on a near daily basis, otherwise you will have to grow wings and go catch it. Parrots don't stick around for long. It is in their nature to wander. They don't like it very much when it's cold out, either, and neither do I, for that matter!

Hey guys, did you remember to pack the suicide pact? It's in the trunk, don't worry. Good. We had written that suicide pact together as children and now that we were teenagers, we would have to make it real some day. We just weren't sure when. We wanted our teenage mass suicide to be fun, but also appropriate. For that reason, we want Jesus H. to be with us.

That's not a parrot, that's a black crow. Get that black crow away from this vehicle. I don't wanna ride the lightning tonight. Is the sky trying to tell us something? Lukas takes out a metal pipe, jams it in his ear. Scream that one more time, into this pipe. I want to feel the words vibrate against my skull. I did what he told me. It's like pornography, he says.

You don't believe in yourself enough to do this. To go to the nightclub, kill all the girls that used to taunt you in school. Or at least one, to make a symbolic gesture. We don't want to leave the house haunted, do we? I don't respect the authorities enough to make them a mess too big to clean up.

Adam draws a picture. I don't want to look; then it will be a surprise. Lukas and Peter switch positions in the driving seat, almost crash the car into the brick wall we've been driving along all the while. Wait, I thought Lukas was Peter. No, that was never the case, Peter was merely Lukas. They found a double-donged identity in the dump, brought it home to burn in the oven. This all transpired before the tanning salon incident.

Let's go on a roadtrip to the end of the world.

We will suicide together holding hands, and thus evade death.

I don't even want this novel to end.

Thankfully it hasn't even begun.

Oh and it never will.

I looked over at Adam's drawing paper and it was full of mustaches. The disembodied mustaches looked so real, a fly landed on one of them and began to lay eggs. That mustache belonged to a real motorcycle man. The motorcycle man is riding after us. We have to escape. He knows that we want to kill the world, so he thinks he'll be a hero and try and stop us. He's watched too many goddamn hollywood movies. He doesn't realize that in real life, the villain always wins. Goodness never triumphs over craftiness. Chasing after us like that just gives me an erection.

I once thought of myself as one of the good guys too, then I met Zach who blew my mind across fifteen continents all at once. At the gas station, the window cleaner queefed into her own milkshake. Suddenly we were in a landfill with imaginary features. Mom, I don't want to go to Texas. There are too many limitations there. It's like its own country too, just like the house I grew up in.

Did motorcycle man fall off yet? I want to see the pink sparks that shoot up when his leather jacket slides across the highway. You know how much it costs to get another one? If every individual were to practice their own version of democracy, we wouldn't live in one. Where we're going, there's a female dictator who makes all the rules.

A messed-up umbrella was found floating in the sewage. Lukas pulled it out. He needed a present to give to his dead GF. The umbrella had a leopard on it. For some reason he thought this would help it fit inside her.

There's medicine in the tampon of my ears. Full-bodied forcefulness clean up the backseat before someone slides back there. We almost got into an accident all because of motorcycle man's hollywood gadgetry, but I know that there's a better day in store for all teenage whores. Silence means it's the end of the song. Or it could be the song itself…

Don't let the dashes shooting out of motorcycle man's engine confuse you. They are just flaccid lights, they have no lasers embedded within. He is just doing it for effectuality. We have planted fleas in his mustache so he will never catch us.

Sometimes the future tastes nice. You have to be disciplined about it, though. You can't just let the schizo take over the entire nipple-biting scheme. The dwarf's entire family could come out of the porno to chase us down the highway. I don't want to go to war with a bunch of midget porn stars, do you? There are comets in your eyeballs, Adam—erase that last mustache, I don't like it.

He was thirsty, so he stuck a plastic cup out the window to collect some rain. Jupiter felt closer than where we were going. It didn't matter; it was only a fox. The borders are opening up, they are represented by red curtains. Men with machine guns are frying lobsters in the kitchen. This house became theirs when we abandoned it. Follow the course of this house through its abandonment, you won't get any interesting stories out of it. You'll only find out how loose the floorboards were before the collision with the dumpster occurred.

We're bringing Adam back to the zoo he escaped from. It's because of the mustaches he's drawing, we don't like them. Oh shut the fuck up Lukas just drive the car. You need to get us there before the sun turns purple and my skin begins to melt. You're an asshole, Matthew, nuclear meltdown is such a last century notion. A mercy blackout is better than getting a blowjob from the mustached stallion.

The Whore wears a t-shirt advertising a popular beach resort she's never been to and a white denim miniskirt with numerous stains of a questionable nature. She wants to offer us something. She gives us a smile that has no teeth. She's a teenager just like us, so we let her in the car.

When Adam's around girls, he can't talk proper. So then the squeaking got even worse. Love is a two-fisted bicycle seat. Which continent y'all headed toward. Anyone you don't have a visa for, baby. I might be a saint, but I ain't got a name. That's all we wanted out of you: to hear you admit that while sweat dripped from the windshield.

We let her out at the next reststop without killing her. Why do you have such an emotion, Peter, I want you to know how good the spectacle tastes when it's been inside you, okay? In the reststop restroom, Peter found his father holding his dong over a pissoir. Oh dad, can we get emotional now all over each other tonight?! Well gee, I don't know son, sometimes it hurts to be me. You'll understand one day too, when an alien comes out of your wife's twat on your wedding day. Peter stuck his tongue in his father's mouth. Thank you so much for teaching me a lesson I never thought I deserved.

One source of light is the window. Another is the rain. Another is the lampshade. Another is the sky. A nun runs in front of our car. He wears a fur collar and forgot how to sing. Zach stopped the car just in time, made a U-turn, drove us back into the broken computer. Now we have a third reason to thrive. Mordant plasticity.

Once there was this girl who believed in something. We pulled up in the driveway, no more transportation of excess. Lukas set his knife down in the empty passenger seat. Zach ran in to fetch the laundry. Saxophone on the radio. Stealth is such a filthy word. Afterwards we'll drive our car into the canal. I know you're evil when you look at me in that way. Stay focused on energizing the banana, Adam squeaks.

Monday comes I feel like hallucinating. Why are we back at the house again? I thought we were on a journey. Beware of flying objects. The floating church meant to transmit the truth, but it got all caught up in optics. Never a flower.

Adam told the world stories, they didn't want to listen. So he became a silent pop star instead. Skullfucked drifter doesn't want to invent himself alright.

Back out on the highway, we ran into the teenage whore. This time she wore no t-shirt, waved as we passed her by. Should we stop the car, give her a ride somewhere. I can't be forced to make these decisions on my own. Adam stuck his head out the window, began to bark at the wall. The wall stuck its finger in Adam's frilly hair, oh that feels so good don't you just want to bite it. Where are we going, says Lukas. I thought we were going to the zoo, I say. No, says Zach, who is driving now, I say we're going to the other continent. Oh fuck, says someone.

If we're going to go on such a long journey, then we need to stop somewhere and get a TV for this car. I cannot go to another continent without bringing a stained TV with me. On screen, a savage Indian slave boy sniffs opium off a knife. There is still some glory left in the world. A nun gets slaughtered in the amazon, the tribe don't recognize her garb. There are planetary reasons for this. Cannibalism is only for special occasions. Somewhere I'll wait for dawn.

Adam's in the backseat re-writing the words to our teen suicide pact. He needs to get it just right before we all sign. The compulsion to fly, the compulsion to smoke cigarettes. Disaster disorder, Zach staring at the reality TV as he drives. The car eats up dotted lines. It is Adam's parents' car. We stole it and we will never return. I need to go to the bathroom.

Whore climbs into the front seat, gives Lukas head while Adam bones her from the back. Zach rolls down the window to eliminate the stink that arises. I hope to turn that television set into a mobile bathing unit, but have to wait until my favorite reality finishes. Mama always used to watch The Price is Right while she played with her titties, says the Whore as Matthew sticks it in her behind. Once she lost a bet with Uncle Cletus and had to eat the trailer.

The Whore smoked a cigarette and led a discourse around tragedy. At one point, Zach mistook Lukas's boner for the driving stick and shifted into the wrong gear. We all lurched forward, Matthew even further into Whore's anal cavity, and crashed through a fast food restaurant that really had no business being there in the first place. In the back seat, we found a new animal—half-chicken and half-crab, it waddled into Adam's orifice and sang a beautiful melody:

> *Grapevines for sweety*
> *Strawberries on her teeth*
> *If you want to marry*
> *Pluck the feathers off my spleen*
> *And set me free*

Oh that was so beauteous, the Whore had eyes. Please let me just freshen up before you tear me apart any further, I want to look good when my maker divorces me.

They were all just dolls, you decide, those angelic people that satisfied your lightbulb yearnings. Now it gets dark and the ride gets faster. It's all black and yellow, the way the road works when you shout down at the asphalt. Lukas screams for five minutes without inhaling once, his face leaning out the window the entire time. The Whore recites a poem.

You know what strikes me, says the Whore suddenly: I haven't had any children yet. I want to go to Vietnam, she says, growing bored. I can't offer you this relapse. The flower-shaped drug went drifting out the window. She busted the windshield with her thoughts.

Get out of my car, shouted Zach, pulled over. We don't have to pay for that either because we took you farther than you've ever been. Wouldn't have gone nowhere, just standing back there all black and sacred. Please, she protested, let me just tell you a story. I know you'll like it. They drove off. She told it anyway, even though there was no one there to hear.

Have we found Jesus H. Christ yet? I think he flew into your brain, you nimwit. I would have definitely noticed, had that happened! I don't think you would. You're so tired these days. I dropped out of high school because of the insinuations. A lot of institutional settings make my breasts hurt.

They drove on, or at least they pretended like they were driving. I drifted off into a place I'm not allowed to tell you about, lest you get the wrong idea about this blue plastic garbage bag I'm always wearing on my head. The only thing that woke me was the sound of the telephone ringing—a sound that I always confuse with the dull hum of running water. Some people never get a chance to pray.

CHAPTER 3

On their way to the land ruled by the
female dictator,
the Suiciders
get trapped
in TVLand.

A dam was applying perfume to his hairline with a q-tip. Let's go kill someone and write a song about it. Stick a knife inside that silence. My hair hurts. Stalin on the TV screen.

Here comes a stale bird. Hey Matthew your cousin's on TV. Matthew's cousin was a famous rapist. The pain of not-being.

Pig falls off the mountain. Conjure a world and put it away. There we were in TVLand, getting raped again.

Matthew's nazi lover was out getting waxed when Arnold banged on the door. Hi Arnold, come on in, Matthew said. Arnold had a bullet and some glass stuck in his throat. Sniffing whiteout, Peter heard, can make you intelligent.

I want to fondle the constellation. A photograph of myself taped to the TV screen reminds me of the world I come from. A world where teenagers don't have hair.

Arnold you have to tell me why you're here. I'm afraid of having another incident like the one last time. Arnold removed his bone needle from my eye socket. What you lack is discipline. Meanwhile Adam found a new father.

I'm used to getting abused by people who can't even spell my last name. Full-throttled diffidence choking down on the radiator's penile loss. Zach entered the space. Zach you can't come into TVLand unless you have the right visa. Fuck a potato, if you ask me one more time, I'll scotch-tape your ear to the wall. I only want to play fair, Zach. As though I knew what fair meant…

Adam came dashing in, moaning incoherently, a large plastic trash bag filled with eyeballs under his arm. Where'd you get those eyes you goddamn fool? They came out of the owls we caught. The animal traps in the woods. We laid them out there to catch food. Embedded them with cameras to see if we could capture any UFO landings. The owls ate the cameras, but at least we got their eyeballs instead.

He plugged his guitar into the amp and started to play a song. Strap broke and guitar fell on his foot. Adam howled like a murdered hound. Then he bemoaned the absence of psychology.

Peter, are you finished getting raped yet? I need you in here next to me.

Zach's soul got cracked. Peanuts flowed out of his skull. An animal came.

This is sooo shady americana in the new millennium. Confusion runs deep into the cracks. The janitor came to clean up our mess. How long you been working in TVLand, black man? Since the lord shot me in the face with his peanut butter gun. Lawlessness is the thing I predicted back there; no one thought there was grass in any of my predictions.

Kung fu warriors invaded Peter's rape sequence. Isotopes shot out of his armpit, landed directly in my eye. I fashioned a new eyeball for myself out of tinfoil and sandpaper. The center of the eye is made of rubber. So if you shoot me in the iris, the bullet will bounce back and go up your nostril. There is no wanky silence.

My hair hurts. Someone said that Hitler got a sex change, was currently living in Mexico. Memory is less dependable than the whore. After getting raped, Peter decided to change his name to absence. Pussyfried petunia sprouts out of desert crevice.

A song in another language comes on the radio, everyone sings along. When we got back from the continent, we were all thirsty for less living. No one had a name. The Whore came over to tell us something about ourselves. You are so brave for entering the premises like that. The Whore went off with the janitor and started a new legacy. By the time it was over, I had already been raped twice.

Don't worry, guys, this is only a broadcast simulation. The real broadcast happens when you're already asleep. It feels so good to have no energy. That way I know I'm doing something correct. Dream last night that I had to undergo multiple castrations until they finally got it right. The magical thing about Arnold is that his urine tastes like an ice cream sundae.

Matthew jumped on a pony and rode on out of there. Yee haw, he cackled as the stars burnt up in the sky high above him. God gets jealous of people with such nice hair. Peter sold all of his to make a carpet. Certain people don't care about things.

Do you want to escape my chunky butthole rape? Then you will have to grow wings and fly high in the sky like Jesus H. you'll never die. Jesus came back to us, you see. She always comes back when she wants more brains. We went into the forest, caught her a possum, and now she munches on his cerebellum with a kind of salubrious joy. She even taught Adam a thing or three about dignity.

Scientists discovered hairs on the planet Neptune last week. Adam picks up his bass guitar and plucks out a bluegrass tune. Matthew grabs the mic and begins to holler. A bunch of pigs come busting through the windows, eliminating this reality. Zach screams as the pigs trample him. When he is done getting raped, he will have a new name.

Hi Peter, how did the wax job go? He's a nazi up on top, but down in his underwear, he's a punk rocker. Geraniums on his t-shirt form a nipple arrangement. The radiator sings a soothing song. It threatens to compete with the pig hollerin' bluegrass arrangement Adam and Matthew are proffering up, so Arnold comes in with a shotgun and blows the radiator away. It makes the sound of a gramophone needle scratching a record as it explodes.

A fist in my morphology. Adam can you come over here please and write your phone number across my face. Eliminate the cloud. A memory collapses inwards, the spatial brain. Envelope opens up, you dump a bunch of sawdust in, seal it, and stick it in the mailbox. The letter will arrive in Alaska before next Tuesday.

Peter has a cunt stuck to the side of his head. He decides to sing a song.

Some feral dust flitted on to the side of his face as he glanced at the upside down convex mirror. Zach had gone upstairs, where he put on every single piece of clothing he could find, then rolled himself down the stairs. Adam farted so hard, the chair he was sitting in broke. The little toe on his left foot had someone's wedding ring on it.

Let's go on a journey to the end of the world. We will kill everyone who gets in our path. That's the message just transmitted by the ceiling fan.

Zach, take all those clothes off right now. I want to see you without skin.

The dark invader. Is there a zoo in TVLand? He lasso'd the radiator, crashed it through the TV screen. A bunch of midget porn stars came streaming out like tears on that TV's shattered face. The cow walked into the laundromat and asked for a sex change operation. I want your hair in my amplifier. Beagles barking into a microphone.

Adam took out his saxophone and began to blow a riff. Angels sat satisfied, the forest fire having abated. Zach began to dictate the logic of desire. He wanted us to go somewhere. We kept thinking about zero. Whore sat down next to me, asked for a light. It was TVLand, so I could put her on mute for a little while. Don't talk to me about who you wish to be.

A cross between a goldfish and a golden retriever. That's the sort of animal I'd like to have as my own. I would scotch-tape it to the wall and feed it dustbunnies whenever it barked too loud. Zach sang a song I don't like very much, so I exited the scenario.

I can deal with my own filth, I just don't want to mutilate someone else's. Matthew smokes out the window of fear. I'm obsessed with Adam. Adam is obsessed with Matthew. Matthew's nazi lover. Peter is obsessed with Zach. Zach is obsessed with himself. A stain on the monitor. We can't tell who the real prisoners are anymore.

Penis is a humidifier. Ankle bracelet handles doom rather well. Peter offers a critical commentary on the nature of defeat while a live mouse tied to a string dangles out of his left nostril. I was in the kitchen trying to remove the castle sticker from the refrigerator with a butcher knife. Accidentally cut myself when Zach came in to recite the pledge of allegiance backwards.

Humility can take many forms. Notionality in a red room painted black. I just cut myself with my favorite album. Where intention isn't pure, you should hand it a microphone.

Adam knew the drawer was haunted because of the version of himself it always displayed. He'd gotten kicked out of school because he wouldn't stop making noises. They thought about giving him a test, but changed their minds. Now he's lost permanently in TVLand, and no one except for us knows where to find him. Promulgate species distrust until the ashes finish him off.

I just shat out a brand new magazine rack. It contains all the latest offerings. You can tell it's a relic from the days when people had genuine obsessions. Not to become all crankified outside of time, like Matthew over there. He has a mohawk and no friends. That's because his nazi lover's pubic hair has formed its own symphony orchestra.

Matthew's friends ran away from him. I don't like it when the sky turns black. It reminds me of my lost parrot. Can you come over here and squeeze my eyeball until it juices?

He climbed out on to the balcony, called out for his friends. His friends were already there. They were warriors, they knew how to cream. A noteworthy incident was the padlocked chain containing all our musical equipment. We had to sing a song to get the danglers unhinged enough to return us to our forebears.

I'm so excited to be seen in public tonight. The vision I have of you in my eye is different from the one in my mind. I don't know which one is more efficient, what I can trust. You offer one truth to the ceiling, the other to your pet shark. Adam writing in his notebook. Let's go swimming before darkness fades.

Red is a color that has no reality of its own. The wife of Arnold's mother just shot herself in the face. I have so many friends.

TVLand is so much better than the WWW. I need world. I'm fried inside myself tonight. There are so many warblings out there to satiate the hunger that de-defines your spite version. I need a hammer. I will only go into the water if I am holding one. Me and Adam are holding hands as he writes this. I whisper in his ear that it's okay to lie.

The cops came to take Matthew away because he was constantly trying to stick his finger into other people's eyeballs. He hid from the cops in the washing machine. I didn't know he was still in there when I stuck the shower curtain in. Matthew you can come out now, unless you want to get real clean!

The cops drove away in a stolen tractor trailer vehicle. We called some other cops to arrest them, and a real cop chase was on—the cops chasing the cops. Some other cops came to chase them all down. There were no more cops left, so we had a big party till sunrise.

At the funeral of the wife of Arnold's mother, the Whore gave a speech peppered with soliloquy and oinks. It was so moving, Arnold's mother nearly fell in the grave too. I kept thinking through the meaning of salvation in order to stay awake. I hadn't seen any birds for a real long time. There were snakes and monkeys all right, but that doesn't mean you can awaken them.

Not much has changed since then. Matthew's reading up on how to build a bomb. Arnold went to his neighborhood tanning salon, got real lost. I'm stretched out on the sofa allowing Adam to snip my toenails. There's some frost on the windows in the shape of a pea. People yearn to pretend and it makes me sad, to be frank, their illusions. So much of it was recycled into teenage memories.

Zach was in the kitchen wearing a halloween mask, trying to shove a metal pipe up his ass. This is gonna take me to the stars, he barely asserted. I got angry and called him a liar. You're supposed to be leading us, Zach. We want to go to the land ruled by the female dictator. You've got to get us out of the TV, or else the sulphur will nullify our mindspan. I can't do everything, Zach snapped, clearly hurt that I hadn't acknowledged how raw he had become in the past nine months. Come on, guys, Matthew interrupted from the doorway, please don't get an emotion right about now.

Arnold grinned in the salt laboratory. He had found a new sanctuary to call his own, thereby writing himself out of the story. A prisoner of his own inhibitions, just like everyone secretly wants. Attainment can be fatal for the fingerless ones, their bones having spun a eunuch's tornado. But there are also bones in the afterlife for the birds to play with. Those birds that carry knives in their beaks and bark out loud at the heavens that entrap them so listlessly.

Peter's whiteout-sniffing had impelled an intervention among us. We intervened one day when he was on the toilet. Peter this has to stop. It will in fifteen seconds he said. No we mean with the thing that makes the pink spots appear. Are you allergic to substance? We had no choice but to throw him out the window, his pants still around his ankles. Dead, he couldn't sniff no more.

We had two less friends, two more than we wanted. It was amazing that Matthew had learned how to count after all that time. On his way into the kitchen, he offered me a popsicle. Peter rang the doorbell to announce that he was still alive. We pretended to be impressed. Who wants to have a milkdrinking contest.

Matthew ate a muffin. I'm sorry.

CHAPTER 4

One of the Suiciders gets moved from the
House to the Home,
which is located on the
Other Side
of TVLand.

Then one day they came and took me away to the Home. I didn't want to go there; I had no choice. People said things could only get better. I knew it was a lie. They just wanted me to do exercises.

As soon as the car took off, I fell out. They had my arms strapped up, so I could only try and crawl after them, wormlike. Wait! Wait! Don't you want to institutionalize me? They changed their minds and drove backwards, running over my face along the way. But that face belonged to another, so I was all right with their definition of identity.

Then it became my job to affirm what everyone else knows. Zach called out to me at night, we're gonna come break you out of that Home. I said I don't want to go back. By then it was too late to sing. Sluttiness is such a teenage tendency, and so is estrogen. Turn off the TV if you want to record me.

Adam mourned the loss of Arnold. He was so sad, he didn't want to suicide no more. Zach did everything he could to cheer him up, even punched him in the face, but all for nothing. Matthew spunked in Adam's hair. Bats attacked it. Horror movie theme plays as Adam ties guitar strings around a baseball bat. Loophole sphincter is benevolent.

Home is like a jail, only with more hairless ones. They allowed me letters from time to time. The first one I penned was addressed to Adam's pet spider. I wanted to tell him everything I felt, which was nothing much at the time. It turned out to be a ten-page letter. All my fears came out of my fingernails that night.

The days were tough and onion-textured. In the mornings we were required to wake up. I had a tough time with this at first, given that we were also made to sleep standing up, but I soon embedded the routine into the nether regions of my skull-fucked latherings. Our mind instructor was a friendly gay man. At least he was thin. He said he would train us how to be free. Plastic horses could be found in the sandbox. I want all the animals in the world inside me now. A film with no antagonists.

It was in the Home I got the idea to change the names of all the countries in Europe. I was wearing a spandex t-shirt at the time. I had a friend in the Home. His name was Rand. Rand hated the Home nearly as much as I did. We spoke often of this, our hatred. We nearly thought we were the same. Then one day Rand let me know how different we were. He came while I was sleeping, tied me down, stuck a sock in my mouth and his penis up my butthole. That's when I found out who I really was.

Now that Rand was not only my friend but also my rapist, I couldn't wait to get out of the Home. They put me in a pink plastic room, left me there for a few days. You could hear a pianist practicing scales constantly in the nearby. I called out, fearing rescue. What happened to all the others, those others who had come to define me in waking life.

Me and my friends, we had made so many plans in that other world, it makes me sad to think of them now. We were going to go on a rape holiday, see how many people we could kill before the animals ate us. We were going to drive to Europe and see how many places we could defile and conquer. I think if we had been more discreet and medieval, we could have made it on to the six o'clock news. Being famous inside your own head can block the blood vessels. Pretty soon you're flying.

They finished shaving Rand and swung him over in my direction. Eat some of this blood, Rand declared. I stuck my fist against his ear, he wailed and wailed. Flowers sprouted. You could almost see a reason for being there. It wasn't fair of me to say that. Where are all my friends.

Wednesdays at the Home were devoted to doing chores. That kind of thing makes me feel so precious and dignified. Rand remained in bed all day eating tomatoes and orgasming under the covers. His offense was killing his own grandmother. I had merely robbed a bakery. Still, we found out we had much in common. We just couldn't trust each other, that was the problem. We each regarded the other as the world's worst criminal offender. Even though neither of us had done very much. In retrospect, it all makes sense now. Rand was jealous of my hair, I was jealous of his hairlessness. If only I had offered him my shavings, we would have been so much closer. It is best not to reminisce on those things in life that may have interfered with fate.

I look out the window, see a cat. This causes me to bang my head against the wall until the friendly gay doctor comes and bitchslaps me back into this submissive reality that is meant to cohere. The way the sun molds the shadow of the building into an obtuse charm, it is like a fuck factory I was never invited to work in. Old timey record gets played on the gramophone in my distress. There are some victims worth fighting for.

Ideas roasted in the left hemisphere of my brain. What I would do when I finally got out of the Home. How far sideways I'd have to squirm once the shocks had finally been cut off. They injected a substance into my neck, made all thoughts disappear for the evening prayer. A hard-on happens once I finally stop feeling. We will hit the road, disappear. The authorities never able to find us, so spineless and wormlike will be our crawlings. Me and all my friends, not counting Rand. Rand is Home friend. Rand'll be in here till the end.

Rand played the skin flute in all his benign wanderings. A melody he learned the day his grandpa passed away. He just wanted to be free, and so he handcuffed himself to the radiator immediately after he slayed grandma. He was too young to be considered a person, so he got to go to the Home. This is where he is taught to choose what kind of self to have on a daily basis, in between meals and prayers and nose-pickings.

Will Rand suicide one day like me and my friends? I don't think he knows who he is hard enough. A blanket lies on the back of his feet. You have to be tender with the animals, it is one of our rules. Even the ones you eat. Even the ones you fuck. Even the ones you kill. You have to be tender with them, or they will fail to buy you.

I want to eat everyone I know. I've already begun. Friendly gay doctor comes in to tell me a secret. I yearn for all that's been lost, everything I can't explain. How come there is no aquarium in this Home. I must write a letter to Lukas, tell him what Zach said in the conversation we had in my head. Are you against the stereotype?

Teenagers fuck so often, they must really want to learn something. Next time Rand fucked me, I told him to slide it in me sideways and sing Billy Jean. What are your goals in this world, asked the doctor as he tongued my balls. I wanna go country line dancing once before I die; the animals.

You have to be discreet if you want to slur my name into the distant network. I have no feelings, either. There is only full-scale war to keep our leaders distracted from doing any real work. Here comes an army of no one. Tell them they are doing the right thing before you send them off to die. Paint their toenails magenta and sing them tender lullabye. Me and Rand will do all the work if you pay us to leave. We only want what's best for the western world which falls apart directly in front of our faces every time we close our eyes for a moment of solace.

Feel the entropy bleating against your spine. The hairless ones encircle us, chant the evening prayer. My confusion your reality. I can't get Lukas out of my eyelashes. As soon as I get out of here, we'll go on a journey to end the world. I want to put an end to all suffixes. A certain primal need to be rubbed out as soon as the fish done frying. I'm so glad you guys came and helped me at the exact right moment, I really owe you so much of my living expenses from the last life.

If you think life is expensive, try getting born. I almost deserved to. I can't ride out of here like I'm a machine on backwards. A moment of being makes me sick. Rand and I sat down to play cards. The three of diamonds had a sticky bit of grime in the corner, so Rand was unable to continue. It took three men to chain him up, all because of a little bit of grime. Oh my catastrophic misfortune, I must get out of this Home before it turns into my own.

The next day we had a seminar in which we had to look at photographs of the insides of people's throats. Something about gravity, I'm not sure. Gay friendly doctor cornered me in the hallway. What happened to Rand, I demanded to know. He stuck his tongue in my mouth and enlightened me. That's when I knew that they had put Rand under the floorboards.

Come hairless warriors, come rescue me from this feeling of abandonment. Entrapment and abandonment are nearly the same. Adam said to kill all emotions. How come I never think of Matthew and Peter while stuck in here. It is because I know that Matthew and Peter are not thinking of me out there on the outside. There are nuts and feelings, boats too. I wish to be buried at sea.

Rand fell down on top of me, the nurse shot him. I got up and inhaled the dustbunnies floating up from his corpse. God-damnit why'd you have to ruin my memory, I shouted. Friendly gay doctor was all over the dead one. Thought he could make him immortal, the horny bastard. Hairs grew sharp as razorblades on his corpse. There is almost a season ready to satisfy us yet.

My favorite thing in life is to be left alone. This leads to social instability on all fronts. Dead flea floats in the beer. How come nobody wants to drink it. I think I know something about you. Sometimes there's so much to do I get frustrated by only having three hands. Must cut the others off.

Rand shat in the morning fog. There wasn't so much to say, and so he went away. Nurse caught him milking someone else's cow, for which the punishment was severe. You ruined my heartache, you empty bastard.

It makes me so happy to think of your lifeless corpse a mangled beauty. Things would be so much better here if you wouldn't stay away so long. My fantasy is to jerk off in the same room as you without you looking or being aware of it. Rats eating something in the corner. Rand comes over and puts a switchblade in my mouth. I want you to tie all the bedsheets together now. I did what he told me. By the time we got the window open, doctor wasn't so friendly, but still gay. He told us that we'd all get shattered if we tried one more thing. I said I know what you mean bro but this here lunatic made me do it, I can't help that I can't make anymore friends in this here institution. Get out of my face. Release me from my own victory.

I missed Matthew all of a sudden. It came on like a tsunami, fears swinging in a hammock. There was no escaping the confines of the Home. Rand would only rape more grannies. The trend-seeking thermometer fanatics hogged the TV room at all hours, I couldn't even see my friends from the distance of the screen. Barbed wire on my fickle victory.

It was getting grainy and hornlike, this image. Had to crash on through, get to another. Be born again just to die at the knife of a molten one. Measure worth by the size of a toothbrush. I had a vision of Adam at home banging a snare drum, moaning. Asphyxiation by fire, the shield. Sadomasochistic reality farm. Living is just another way of saying dying.

There is such joy in seeing you fear. The hairless ones falter. My idol has always been one I hardly think about, all lackluster and gray. Are you facing the truth or are you merely mutilating it? I can't thank you hard enough.

Some curtains were drawn over the slab of the wall that Rand had painted. They didn't want to influence the other teenagers in the Home. None of them were my friends. Without them, I couldn't know who or what I was. By then I had given up on communicating with friendly gay doctor for fear of being molested further. His brand of therapy something I was only too used to in the external world—still, I didn't want it, not from the Home. I wanted something else. To download a new value system into my skullsphere. Nothing happens when you're naked and the world is aware.

I knew the other Suiciders would be off practicing without me. There would be new songs to learn, other hopes to defeat. Thoughts of breaking out, previously a mere component of my dehydrated fantasy life, became more frivolous. I thought about drinking something that would land me in the hospital.

But the outer dudes also had their ambitions. Ambitions I'd end up being proud of them for. They were gonna come get me out of there, I just knew it. I summoned the energy to care for a moment or three. Once we were in the car of Adam's parents, I took my dick out to show them the nose tattoo. Adam had already forgotten that I was there. He was so busy inscribing all his lusts into the tablet. I waved goodbye at Rand, who shot me a meaningful grimace. A grimace that said he wanted to rape me once more before all his fears ran away.

What I learned from the whole experience is that you have to grow into exile. Hairlessness is a state with no country, an end without a beginning. Once you learn to love it, you will also learn how to mutilate it. Matthew was dryheaving in the front seat. Peter can I drive this car? I want to feel so free, you can't even imagine...We drove past an abandoned lampshade factory. Let's get out there and eat some popsicles. There is work to be done.

We ran over someone's fur-coated reality on the way back to our real home, the House: I forgot to tell you we burned it down while you were away. Now we have nowhere to take you; that's why we decided to get you out. What? Stop making sense. No, it's because we need a leader now. And you want me to be your leader? I'm so flattered by this genuine act of friendship. Get the hell away from me, it stinks.

Deep inside my mind, there are three tiny men arguing. Each of them are me, yet someone else's version of me. I was so happy to be surrounded by my friends again, I wanted to tell them something. Instead I gave them all new names. Then we drove to Europe where we could feel free once again.

Matthew became Marc. Peter was Phil. Phil was Lukas. Zach was Jill. Adam was Aesop. Arnold was dead.

We stopped on the corner to pick up the Whore. She had lost another tooth while I'd been away. Y'all lookin for a good time. She didn't recognize us. Hey baby we're gonna take you far far away from here. Get ready to lick my cryptic eyeball.

She climbed in the back, started unbuttoning her jeans. That's when she knew. I thought you guys might be interested to know, she began. My new pimp works at the zoo. Me and Adam looked at each other. I had already forgotten everyone's new name.

CHAPTER 5

The Suiciders,
a rock band for animals,
must go on a journey in order to remain
teens forever,
though they're not quite sure how to do this,
and so they ask their good friend Jesus
for advice. The Suiciders go to Adam's house to
kill his parents so that they'll have
a crime to run away from.

F reaks speak a language of their own sadness. The time
comes to buy a shotgun. Now that Zach had finally gotten a chance to learn who his friends really were in this life, it
was time to kill them all. He put on a Harry Pussy CD and
tried to sing along, there weren't a lot of words, there weren't
a lot of things he had to say, either. But there was the noise—
that stupidity and anger—there was the monster truck driver
he had stuck his thing in the night before—there wasn't a lot
of attachment—not of the artificial sort, at least—he wanted
to produce art that referenced nothing. This was Peter, the
glue-sniffer.

If your art goes too far outside of reference, Peter, people might mistake it for something else. An ant, for instance. I don't give a fuck about anything, I just want to stick a lightbulb up my anus. Your version of containment gives me relief from the fire that burns in shards of rain all around us. Adam wrote his will down in a spiral notebook, then threw it away. The will of the people will never be absolved.

Zach's shitter had never been fucked before. He had no desire to be gay. As an experiment, he went to the local gay bathhouse, found the man with the biggest dick there, and got him to stick it up him. He ran home, laughing all the way. Now he's done everything sexually that he never wanted. So he can finally be free. Freedom is a delusion. Set all newspapers on fire. I don't want to see anymore.

Peter kept on making his art inside the bathroom. He'd sit in a tub full of noodles all day, fantasizing that they were really waffles. He took a butcher knife and sawed his head open. All sorts of insects crawled out of that. If you think he's deluded, you should meet my mother. Here let me go dig up her corpse as you read this, crying.

He once made a mandolin out of electrical wires, then plugged em all in as some poor sap tried to play it. His fingers were fried inside the stapler. Armageddon comes in thirty-three flavors—just the sort of massage the pope wants. This is not a space for ruining other people's art.

Peter's running down the hallway, his head hanging halfway off, trying to keep it up with a string. Hey guys I think I discovered a new foundation want a taste of my yogurt? Put your goddamn head on your shoulders or you won't go with us on the journey, Zach commanded. Oh what is this now being supreme leader has gone to your head? I just got out of a goddamn mental institution, I don't have to subjugate my consonance to your blather-in-law. Let's mutilate all vowels before salvationtime is thrust on us once again, Lukas interjected. You just want to lick my magnificent buttcrack, admit it! Now don't go singing victory birds here, buster, I'm the sort of creamer you would never dignify via long-term divestment.

All the friends are here again. Matthew is satisfied.

Here comes a smelly rose no one wants to think about. She drives a car. She won't go far.

The friends commit a murder together they must go away. They will take a roadtrip to all thirty-nine continents. That is their goal at least. Along the way, they will have some adventures. But they won't talk about it with no one, for fear of disrupting the purity of each passing moment as it rapes their veins.

That ungodly tornado I don't understand whosoever will I fuck tonight?

Jesus H. flew on my shoulder. Squawked a sentence in my ear. Hey you guys Jesus H. thinks we should burn the house down before we abandon it. You know. To make things complete-like. We can't do everything that goddamn bird wants us to do. Hey Adam you know nothing about the animal kingdom. I know what a spider looks like when it is trapped inside someone's armpit.

It's a good thing they're talking. Suicide silence hearkens collapse. Attack of the neverending. Adam's spider crawls into the eye of Jesus. The only times I feel we really understand each other is when you're spitting on me. I'm sorry I made the bridge collapse, mom.

Adam's parents were killed as a result of me stealing their car. They didn't want to let us grow up so I had to bash their heads in. Running around here doing so much work the children begin to wonder. Wonder at the unfilled ashtrays that their grandpa used to shove inside them to learn them wonder and merriment all at the same time. Adam just suicided all over the floor. Peter paints a picture of armageddon.

Zach tells Peter to go hang his work up in an art gallery. Peter denies. He says the truth is a biscuit with a liquid disease spread across. Here comes a shaman banging his dumb ass drum. Since Adam is dead we ask him to join our band. Haven't you ever heard of us? We're the Suiciders. All our fans are animals, living and dead.

Jesus flew over and knocked the shaman right out the door! I've never seen any goddamn thing like it since Peter's python choked on the lightstand three years hence. Do you want an anteater to be the source of your demise? Get away from here Peter you can't be my friend. I don't have enough world in my pocket to start a fight.

Oh the smelly rain, I hate it so, even if it brings good things, such as paranoia and distress and talk about god. Zach comes over with a knife and declaims he's the real god. He just wants to lead us somewhere. We know something about sweet salvation. Adam just grew a mustache. That happens sometimes, when you're dead. Stop, says Matthew, that's my bacon.

The western world eats my shit sometimes. The goddamn insects had infested Jesus. We had to take her to the vet to get a new lifestyle. She didn't like the old one, it was full of fleas. Zach comes over with a knife, cuts all the bugs out of her. There's not much Jesus left after that, but we never had much inside us all to begin with.

The society we suddenly found ourselves a part of was the inside of a diseased felon's kneecap. In order to put an end to all inherited notions of justice, we would have to become killers. Killing a loved one is the ultimate transgression, so we thought we'd start with

Adam's parents, who none of us loved, not even Adam. That was our way of taking things one step at a time, prostitute style.

On the front porch, we looked in through the window. There were no lights on. This was going to be easier than we thought. When we went inside, Adam's mother appeared holding a steaming hot cup of coffee in her bathrobe, left tit hanging out. Her tit had a tattoo of a martian lapdancer on it. She flung the coffee all over me, scolding my mind in the process. I hit the bitch upside her head, knocked her down to the floor, screamed hallelujah as I stomped on her face. Jesus came and landed on my shoulder. Adam just stood there watching the whole thing. It was like he had never seen a murder before, even though he had conjured plenty in his dreams on paper.

A zoo is a nice place to have a wank. Plenty of children around on a sunny afternoon in the spring. Sudden flowers impede our movement. We cannot move past them in case they have been imbedded with motion sensors. There are all sorts of gods among us, and they are all equally nameless and fascinating. The trash bin was overflowing, so I went over and sang a song to it.

A day is rotten when too much hope happens, weighing it down. Matthew's friends are all at the zoo, Adam's mother explained to us, lying there with her face half burnt off. Give us the car keys, bitch, said Zach. Oh Zach my mother is not a bitch, said Adam, she is merely a rotten pig cunt. I don't need to clarify my options at this point in the game.

Peter was a sexual addict and had so many friends. He didn't know what to do with most of them at times. They would say something to him and he would look away. Adam's mother is on the floor moaning. She keeps asking for a lamp. In the other room, Adam's father was stuck to the couch. He had given up on movement. I don't want to know who you are now. Give those damn kids the keys woman. You hear what your man said. No that was just the parrot mimicking his voice. For that, Jesus flew over and kicked her in the face. Birds don't lie, woman.

I don't want to beat up Adam's mother anymore I already know I'm crying. Sometimes it's hard to get the keys. We just wanted to be teenagers for the rest of our lives; why was everyone against us so? Molten frustration can be used as a weapon as well, can't it? Here comes an army of bees.

Peter's parents had to take him to the doctor. They found him eating a cardboard cut-out of Spain. He was diagnosed with mutilated self syndrome. There's no psychology, spat Zach. Quit making those pronouncements.

Mutilated self syndrome is what happens when you no longer have any cognizance as to your inner sanctum's whereabouts. The inner gets lost, you go looking for it behind the space heater. You find a cat there and the cat barks like a dog. Pretty soon you are hanging from where the curtains are supposed to be, having become a curtain yourself, and all the neighbors are wondering whatever happened to your hair. Sometimes I'm so ugly I want to cry.

I have a charity event just in case someone tries to ride off on this here primitive butthole explosion. Adam only believes in vowels. He will write an entire book that consists of nothing other than different vowel arrangements. Peter says that's not art. Peter has become a curtain. Matthew jumped into the llama's vagina. He swims through the insides of this dear and tender animal, looking for an elastic idea. I'm right upside myself with knowledge, birds quake softly bimorphic.

Peter's art referenced nothing. That is because he was always on whiteout. He tried to saw his own skull open and paint his brain white. His mother would never allow that. She wanted her son to be normal like everyone else's son. She knew, oh, she knew all right what the future tasted of. She knew so hard she got tired and put on sandals. Peter came crashing through her world. He found his mother seated in the sink. Get the hell out of our house, mom. We're the Suiciders—it's not your spectacle.

Zach was jogging around the house wearing a clothespin on his scrotum and a fake mustache. He thought he was being chased by Jesus, but the bird was nowhere to be seen. Only Zach could see his dear pet. That's what made the moment so authentic in my memory. Oh the days were wild with laughter and ribald gaiety. Then a knife came stabbing through the days, interrupting our fornicatory mission fathomings. Time to kill everything, says Zach in a robot voice.

They were like the rest of the world only something different. A pale pink shadow of doom's distress. That shadow oozed another shadow, hardly lesser than the one before. The two shadows spawned a third in the shape of a cloud. The cloud shadow emitted another shadow in the shape of light. The light shadow gave rise to a lampshade shadow. The lampshade shadow gave birth to Jesus H. Christ the parrot. Now I'm on holiday, he screamed before jumping through the window. God-damnit Adam now shards of glass scattered all over the floor.

Adam came to me with an emotion. I'm so proud of you the way you beat up my mother last night I want to give you this blue trophy. Adam I'm so touched let me break it over your head. I will go perform oral sex on the decapitated corpse.

To be a mess inside your mind. I keep floating angel-like through the dusty light that has come to define this space. Let's go on a roadtrip to the end of the world. I thought the one true story was the one that never got written, said Adam out loud as he wrote in his notebook. I liked you better when you squeaked incomprehensibly into your shirt collar.

Sometimes when I'm on the toilet I have a memory. I went away to the Home and then came back to the House, which had burnt down; still, it was still there. The Home and the House are two different places. You must memorize their locations before both disappear. History wipes our asses like that. A bare lightbulb existence is something Zach always wanted. Zach didn't realize he had so many friends until he looked around him one day and noticed that he didn't know anyone's name anymore. Matthew's planting flowers in the windowsill.

A bare lightbulb existence. So many teens and so little cream. Your face hits the wall, you think you know something. Matthew has a pet orangutan. Peter makes great art.

Does it help you function, to hold me like that? I dove into a world, I witnessed my own collapse. Peter avoids this one by creating his own. That is what all true artists should do, but most of them are bullshit.

You don't need a comb in a bare lightbulb existence. Charity is often hairless. Matthew's friends are running away as I write this. I am Adam today, you can be Zach and Lukas. Zach and Lukas fuck each other; you fuck yourself.

Lukas went down to get some ice cream. When he came back up, Zach was holding his boner in his hands. He waved it back and forth like a magic wand. A fairy appeared. That fairy granted no wishes. That fairy only wanted a french fry. We gave it one, all right, then we kicked its asshole back into the radiator.

I like it when something happens, Adam suddenly said. Being alienated had taught him how to become more coherent.

He has graduated from a squeak to a squawk. I want Adam to become a farmer.

Out the window, a gay scene. The retard girl from next door we used to torture is squirting herself in the face with a garden hose. She laughs ha ha ha it's so funny we're all going to die. Lukas goes outside and sprays her down. She falls and rolls down the hill, shrieking all the while. Then Lukas picks up the garden hose and sprays himself in the face for five minutes. Unlike the retard, Lukas doesn't laugh.

There are so many different ways of being alive now these days, that's the problem, we must limit ourselves. A police officer knocks on our front door. I want to see Zach. Did a retard roll by here? What do you think this is, a collective farm. Smells more like a cheese processing plant. You almost guessed the nature of my disease. Please get out of here, you are disturbing Peter the artist.

Peter had so many friends. He wanted to make art that referenced nothing. Zach ran away from here. He thought he could do it out there in the world without us all weighing him down. The world would teach him something else, that's for sure. I think it's because he got raped so much when he was away in the Home. Now that he's homeless, he should be safe from rape.

The world ass was his best friend. Whenever he vomited, Adam's spider would come to sift through the pieces. Peter is making a new art piece. I want to commit suicide but am afraid I can't afford it. I hope my friends will all be here when it comes time to make a new self-discovery. Matthew accidentally mutilated most of his selves before they had a chance to blossom. Matthew's selves ran away from him and Jesus H. flew right into his braincell. Let's go on a journey, you guys.

CHAPTER 6

The journey finally starts to happen
(again).
Certain dynamics elucidated.
Fat City.
Satan.
The Suiciders get a new member.

They were in the car, chewing wood. The police was after them. At least that's what was written in Zach's field of vision. On the road to forgetting his doubts, Matthew had become a drag queen. Now we're all warriors of a certain ferocious sort.

This is all refined situationality. A situationality that hurts at times. Someone's dog once had wings. Matthew loved Arnold cos Arnold would never do anything to him. They didn't fuck or talk or nothing. They just rubbed brains until one person had gotten off and the other person had run home. Wanting to use drugs, Peter was automatic masturbation. He gave open-mouthed kisses to some of the sailors docking nearby. This day when the sun crashes down to the earth, Peter could see spiders everywhere. They were the spiders in Matthew's brain.

We pulled in to Fat City half past midnight. Lukas had been shot trying to recover our car from Adam's shotgun-wielding father. We rode with his corpse tied up in the trunk. Zach knew a man at

Fat City who would offer us instant salvation at a rock-bottom price. He might also be able to fix Lukas's arm. Lukas didn't want to see no doctor. He'd rather walk around bleeding for the rest of the story.

How proud your mother would be of you on this day Lukas if only she hadn't died and gone to hell. Lukas recalls a time when satirical indifference had done much to fry up his brains. Gay people know no lightbulb. Adam's figurative androgyny there on the paper. Lukas fell out of the car onto the gravel parking lot. He sang a song.

> I've been shot
> Not feeling so hot
> Do you want to see me frown?
> Eat my membranes
> Right out of my nose
> I'm too tough to fall down

That song was so touching that Peter got out a shotgun and blew a hole in his own mouth. The bullet went down his throat and got stuck there. Now we have two reasons to meet a faithhealer tonight.

Inside Fat City, pink metal buzzed through the speakers. One couldn't tell if the speakers were broken or it was the recording. A series of dead anteaters mounted on the wall. They used to have wild animal parties down here, where all the local hunters'd come wearing the heads of whatever they'd killed that day and fuck on the dancefloor. A thousand proper nouns all yearning to be legitimized in a certain fashion. My indignance at the fact that the owner wasn't in there to greet us right away.

But the owner soon came out, all smelling of fried onions and unsaturated fat. He grunted us a welcome you had to be well-versed in the machinations of stupidity to decipher.

There was only one other customer in the bar that night, a trashed-out recluse, went by the name Fricky cos no one had ever been told otherwise. Fricky used to shoot the sperm of raccoons into his arms. Said it gave him a special feeling that no other substance could replicate. Fricky also likes to lick himself when no one's looking. Where is my lover Arnold, Peter suddenly cried out. I thought he was supposed to be my lover you imbecilic waif, cried Matthew in return. Adam fell down on his knees and began to cry. Peter was really Lukas, you see.

Lukas here's been shot; think you can fix him up? The owner of Fat City was spooning some sort of jellified meat into his mouth from a bowl with his shotgun. He was covered in fur and had no teeth. He looked like some sort of wild animal they haven't yet gotten around to naming. But alas he was only a man. A man who knew the value of turning your back on the law and farming out vultures to take care of all the moribund alarmists.

Put your arms around me when you suck me, Fricky said to the wall. He thought it had become alive but alas it was nothing. Some framing device needed to keep it all in there. There are no languages outside of freedom.

The future is a psychopath with AIDS. Adam only squeaks when he is fascinated by something. The owner of Fat City just removed the bullet from Lukas's arm using the teeth he didn't even realize he had. The dead anteaters on the wall hummed in chorus. Show me a picture the inside of your head. A Russian version of myself, says Adam.

Zach snorted something off the owner's knife. Goddamn outsiders coming in here trying to bring us all down: that's what Fricky said, barely audible through the churning vines growing out of the antique Fat City speakers. Owner wasn't about to take any of Fricky's shit: you get on out of here with your raccoon sperm Fricky or I'm liable to call the law on your asshole.

I'm glad we got out of that former place, Zach thought to himself, suddenly melancholic. A fever of dry regrets was making his booty quake. Now I'm thinking you're a sea lion. Feel the sonic vibration of my hatred nastifying under the orange lamp. I am something like a self, unfocused under the trailer. Fricky the fearsome neanderthal wanderer makes his way to the door. On his way out, he burps up a nightingale. That's so pleasant Fricky, says the owner, do you want to borrow my shotgun? Fricky had to go remove his catheter before the angels came to take him up to heaven. Spuds of angels darkly.

Adam took Fricky's place on the barstool and began to write. When Zach went over to look, there were no words on the paper. Only a drawing, a mutant sandal. All the children who were born here in Fat City, said the owner, they all grew up to become deformed visionaries. Their hostility to the external world could be measured with a shot glass. Rather than hate, they learned to objectify the details of their surroundings, a plasticized idiot world, and hence were able to stop many of the attempted robberies on the place. Cos you know, the neighborhood's certainly not what it used to be. I could think of better places to host the world's distress. But I'm not the type to fear movement, you know. I just have to go with it, until the winds blow me into the wild. This here fur's gonna protect whatever strands of innocence still reside on my persona.

Suddenly he turned to Adam. Your mother was a castrated holidaymaker here for many years, I have to admit. Adam wasn't shocked. You mean you know me better than he does? Pointing at Zach. Holy rape survivors oftentimes have memories of past lives coursing through their veins. I will shove this entire notebook inside me if I hear one more word flit past about saviors and lives.

Are you Danish, said Peter.

Oh here comes the Sunday morning rain. I wish I could be a part of this somehow, but I forgot how to squeak. Are you the teenage rapist of my former fantasy? There are some thoughts that can receive no satisfaction. I am one of them: mounting savior rainbow. The teenage pilgrim is nice. You are a douchebag whenever you're not speaking. I don't care anymore. The aggressive verb.

It's a gruesome scene. The elephants went swimming in our pond not realizing there were sharks living in there. The elephants got pulled underwater and munched apart. The agony of noticing that was unprecedented in the history of our little group. We wanted to have total control of all the death around us, but mostly missed out on the thin happenstance that tended to evolve not so lightly. It's amazing how much time it takes to become someone these days. I see a reflection of a former self in the window and ask the owner to let me smash it. We heard a knock on the door and the owner opened it to a friendly biker gang that happened to be passing by.

The bikers all turned out to be hairless, which is quite surprising in this day and age. To not conform to a stereotype is a painful process, but also one that can be quite comforting. Let me show you a picture of my aunt.

The leader of the bikers was a woman with a harelip. She was always there for the other bikers whenever they caught a disease.

A rabbit hopped over to the framework. A telepathic phenomenon not really. Are people who take drugs liars? Go ask Adam something about yourself. Identity doesn't really matter so much in these situations, it's more about excuses.

Cryptic fabulosity yields so much appeal, Matthew told the bikers, here read the bible. We had never read it ourselves, because our teen suicide pact was the only bible that ever really mattered much in the larger scheme of things. I got fat and hairy by touching myself that spring. Peter the whiteout-sniffing art fag taught me how to hold a glass of beer with my foot.

The snake was hiding in Lukas's amplifier. Nobody knew if it had been planted there on purpose or not, but it bit Lukas's elbow off when he tried to play the guitar. His girlfriend at the time was a tense teenage bisexual who could never understand.

One of the local teens came down to Fat City that eve, seeking out new adventures. He went around the bar interviewing everyone about their proclivities. When he got to us, Zach handed him a suspicious glare. I felt so sorry for the child. That feeling ended when I realized that the child had his own version of deliverance to yield.

Taylor, like many of us there that night, had been born. Get out of my house, his mother told him. That's how he ended up at Fat City. There was a train wreck in his brain, you see.

Have you had sex, Zach asked him bluntly. Not yet, but I was involved with a satanic cult. Only those who have undergone the rape initiation are allowed to join the Suiciders. Red spiders crawled all over me, said Taylor, I was just a child, I had no control over my own soul. Fat City is sanctuary for me. All the adults in this town are corrupted, they're all a part of it. My mother's boyfriend is the black wizard. It's your biggest middle american fears all come to life. A suicidal sadness overtook him. Lukas ran over and gave him a hug, so Zach had no choice but to punch Lukas in the face. Lukas fell down and broke his other elbow. There are no eyeballs.

Biker chick came over to teach us all hard firm lesson about gloating. We snorted it up and handed her a rebar for her actions. Don't blaspheme the secret goat before I get out of China. He slapped her back into this parallel reality.

It was a chill, a winter deal. The only way we could come back was to flop backwards—the car had broken down with the corpse still in it. Does Taylor want to join the journey? We can't force him to choose between us and goodness. An evening of shit and sunglasses. The thin endurance festivities were due to begin one hour past daylight savings time.

I fear fearing you, tearing you apart and swinging. In my confusion I mistook Adam for Zach. Now I can't recognize any of my friends. It must have something to do with the food I was given earlier. I just want to go somewhere smooth without singing.

Peter is still seeing Matthew's brain spiders run around everywhere. They run on Taylor's face, leaking blood. Taylor doesn't seem to notice what's happening to him. Maybe that's because he willed it himself. Taylor was born into a satanic cult. They made him become what he is today. Taylor goes to Fat City all the time. The owner is his best friend. He knows the owner, a sleazeball, is the only authentic person in this town, the only one who has not given himself over to the dictates of satan. With someone who is scarcely more than a shadow of a shadow, you can only hope to own them. Where is my mother and why have my friends run away from me.

The sky was his only friend. He had been through so much at such a young age, it was unbelievable. When I look at Peter, I think of Adam. Lukas seems to think otherwise, another direction completely. I believe we accidentally drove to the wrong continent and now there's no vehicle to pull us out of it. The bikers can't help us; they will only transport themselves. I have too much hair to ever join their gang. I don't want to invade someone else's internal logic, if you know what I'm saying. Oblong teen expressionists are on the rise.

A goat came out of nowhere to tell us all about freedom. The bikers reacted with violence, slaughtering the goat and roasting it on a spit fashioned out of ice picks. We wanted to develop the scene even further, but none of us were auto mechanics. Taylor do you know how to fix a car. Maybe you can get us somewhere. If that happens, he can join the journey. But you must understand what it means. When we say journey, we mean ultimate. I think I know a bridge that will lead us out of here. You're on, honey.

Something else he said really impressed me. I don't want to be famous, just honest and putrid. The calligraphy of soullessness can be etched on a grain of rice. A mountain in the foreground collapsed, forming yet another mountain out of its dust. It's a tough world to be a part of, but then most are.

Suddenly an army of throatsinging dwarves appeared on the scene to avenge the death of their porn star father. Quick Adam, shouted Zach, light some candles! It was Taylor who got us out of the way by regurgitating lifeless as a form of salvation. He pulled out his trumpet and joined our band. He was wearing his school uniform. He wanted to assert something.

With all the dwarves dead, Zach clapped him on the shoulder. It's now official; you are permitted to join the Suiciders.

I wanted this to be a special moment, but when I went to sing, I found I had lost my voice in all the meanderings that night. The owner of Fat City came out wearing a pink leotard. He said he wanted to show us something special. Lukas and Matthew went with him around back. When they came back, they were changed teens. I mean literally—they had switched identities and everything. But that's okay, because before, both their identities had been very similar. So this does nothing to disrupt the narrative, now I'm sorry I even mentioned it.

You're so clever and a recluse, doesn't this role get hard to play at times?

They were able to get the car engine rolling again by feeding it a live baby anteater that the Fat City owner was keeping in his bathroom just for fun. That mountain over there, we call her Sally. Once you cross it, you'll be headed in the direction you want to go, he advised. We can only trust verbs that re-articulate nouns. Thanks, someone mentioned.

I don't want a hot dog, I just want a gray house in the suburbs. Some friends to call my own. There are reasons to exist in this day and age. This is what separates us from the past. The filth of days leaking down my forehead. Tiny rocks in an ashtray, but no cigarette ash. In the car, our new member among us, only voiceless feelings to train.

Adam's spider got left behind. When he realized it, he cried a string of silent tears and then ate an entire box of rice pudding. Get over here and name me. It's because it hurts to forget.

We still had Jesus, though, our fears all intact. Jesus H. kept asking us to stop and let her go on a pony ride. We had to keep moving for fear of bumping into the Whore all over again. She wanted us to drive her around to all her favorite fast food restaurants. We feared these goddamn places. We wanted to make money too, just not that way. There are certain things you just can't do with yourself to enliven the process of enlightenment. Peter's mind was shattered into many cute shards. Adam sat back once his tears were dry and began to count the stones he found in the ashtray. Zach is driving this car the way a man knows how. It was when we were already over the mountain that we realized we'd been sent in the wrong direction.

CHAPTER 7

The forest.

A dam's new art form was to shut the fuck up right outside of satisfaction. Twin monuments to someone else's deed appeared steadily on the horizon—we were approaching the wrong destination.

Adam got excited and squeaked so loud he woke up Zach, who was driving. Why'd you do that dingus, I only wanted a reality refurbishment to go.

Taylor, the newest Suicider, was in the backseat trying to clarify things. So you're a teenage terrorist group out to destroy all nouns. Not exactly, said Lukas, strumming his guitar, it's more like we see ourselves as backwards visionaries. We let each and every moment tell us which way to go.

Just then, Adam's arm fell off. The elbow crushed his pet spider, who had been relaxing on the arm rest next to him. The guts of his pet spider flew into Jesus Christ's eye, temporarily blinding her and causing a massive squawk to be emitted from her beak, a squawk that so startled Zach that he ran off the road and into a national forest, where he accidentally ran into a moose. The moose's antlers flew off and bisected a large oak tree, which housed a family of monkeys. The tree crashed to the forest floor, crushing a large anthill and causing a rain of monkeys, one of whom landed on our vehicle, causing the engine to fly skywards and crash into a cloud, causing an enormous rainstorm to explode over all of us, as the homeless ants terrorized the monkeys by seeking refuge in their fur.

Taylor nearly saved us all. But that is what he got born to do. His appearance came at the right time. Kill all nouns, he told the monkeys, kill all nouns. The monkeys listened to him and then they vibrated. Zach told Lukas to go find an anteater to suck on their fur. Adam was busy supergluing his arm back on. The Whore came into the forest, moaning. I think I left my sunglasses in your car. No one wants to pay me without them. The Whore had already become a retard, you see.

My good name is on holiday today. The absence of color made Lukas horny. We were in a black-and-white forest and night was fast on the horizon, meaning we'd soon be blotted out of the story altogether. We had to do something, build a fire, but nothing burns in the rain. Nothing, that is, except for more rain—the type you produce on the ground. An amber-colored shitbox is your mother's caravan. I'm glad we found the gypsies—we could never make love without them here watching.

The Whore went off to gather flowers. She kept them warm by storing them in her vaginal cavity. Adam stuck a firefly nest up his ass to show that he was equal. A thousand squirrels ran over the gypsies, who had begun to shave in solidarity with our raunchy brigade. Taylor was stuck to the roof of the car, screaming. Screaming women don't hallucinate. I left my friends and went walking through the forest. I wanted to get away from the Whore, but also all shadows that might remind me of a previous version of self I once held up as role model to the mindless ones.

I was a mile away before I realized that one of the squirrels that had attacked the gypsies had broken away to follow me. I was so lost in my own drift of thoughts that the squirrel had to bite my ankle to get me to notice it. Once that happened, I nearly lost my temper and stepped on its tail. Instead, I listened to its solution.

We have reached a consensus, it said, and we no longer wish to be called squirrels. We would now prefer the name lightbulb. That's not possible, I said, the word lightbulb is already taken. I'm afraid you will have to think of something else to call your-selves, though squirrel seems to me just as pure as the sun crashing into the ocean.

Just then a bearded man wearing a dress appeared from behind a tree, nearly startling me into a dominatrix-like posture. When I said the word lightbulb, he pointed at the squirrel.

The bearded man followed me back to our makeshift camp. There, Lukas was caught up in painting red dots on Adam's underwear. Adam was reciting Hungarian poetry from the 17th century. I fell on Zach's face and laughed so hard my bladder exploded and drowned all the lightbulbs in piss. Bearded man sat down next to me, snorting. He still hadn't said a word, and the sun had nearly suicided itself into a cloud. I said the word cloud out loud. Bearded man pointed at a blade of grass. When I said the word grass, he pointed at a monkey. He had all the words wrong, and suddenly I didn't give a fuck. I gave the bearded man a hug. A shadow fell across his skin. Taylor came rolling like a cannonball towards us. He wanted to touch the forest floor with his entire body and had apparently succeeded. In doing so, he erased much of himself, but it's okay, now at least we can take the forest with us.

A mustache-shaped mushroom is really a cloud. You could still hear the roar of the highway from three thousand miles away. Zach said, I think I have a plan for evading the midgets. There was no one after us, at least no one affiliated with the law. We only had the trees to battle with. I think Zach was scared because we didn't have an enemy. The man with the beard was dancing on the hood of our car. The Whore ran over and started to beat him on the head with her purse. Take those earrings off, I'll replace them with a tree branch, take them off now.

In certain places the wolves have no brains. Their skulls are a lot smaller and you have to stick batteries up their assholes. They operate like other animals, though, they just have fewer emotions. Taylor sneezed so hard he vomited up a Fat City ashtray he'd stolen. Turned out he was allergic to the forest. It's okay, said Zach defiantly, we're still going to spend the night here. Not only that, declaimed Matthew, I'll be using my penis as a lampshade tonight, thank you very much.

That boy had feelings he just couldn't figure out how to suppress in the right fashion. The forest was filled with graves. No one knew what to say any longer. They soon had a collective fear which the bearded one articulated by pointing his finger southwesterly. The Whore spoke up: My name is Ginger.

The Whore had no name. Therefore she was sad. Sometimes she imagined herself to be proper. But that was only a game. She owned two chainsaws and not much else. Still, she could wander.

The Wandering Whore tried to suck off armageddon when she noticed a key ring. Now the founding fathers don't pray to her. The mushroom in the shape of a mustache came out of the gun. We were so fortunate to be together that night, we found out the true meaning of friendship by getting killed together in the forest.

When the midnight sunburn struck, we could be found running into the blackened enclosure. I don't know what it was that thought it was chasing us. I hadn't a chance to see it, for fear went into my shoulder. Lukas's pine cone vibrator was still stuck in my senior orifice, learning lessons. Adam wrote a letter to the season requesting a disease. I love to touch things I can't control.

I love your life, says the Whore to the rock before vomiting all over it. Zach sneezed and out came the sunrise. It was just like in those movies, where everyone vacates their tent at the same time, to find the pristine orange mauve of the silent new day. A history of satan's legacy in post-colonial Africa.

Some children are born with stains. Others have hominids. They ran through the forest until it was no longer on fire. To be dead is to live in the future. I expanded the gorilla on the way back home. Adam's sinuses got bent over Peter's shit-mining grin. The suicide satellite disappeared behind a river.

I went chasing after it to find myself confronting a small boy, which the bearded philosopher had become overnight. He stood on a bridge waving at the fish swimming by under him. I don't want to breathe the night air. There wasn't much to add. When the little sour boy saw me, I figured he must be stoned. I was shy so he invited me over. Look, we can wave at the fish together. You don't have to worry about the lack of nectar. I thought I heard a truck driving through the forest. A blue light, the days scream.

I took the child with me. The forest humming all around us, a veritable vibration, no more suave pilots, just the two of us finally. Could we ride this thing out together? The path in front of us far from pristine. I felt unright. Swervy though curvilinear in my own regards, the crunchy leaves my sole source of repetition. I couldn't have dreamed any of this far better than it looked. The child began to wallow. I had my back against his face when the gray owl belched spectacular.

Three long thin black things sticking out of the ground. Burnt. They looked like the former foundations of a church, but what were they doing in the middle of a forest, the forest of no names and talking animals. The forest of an entire nation. My soulmate grabbed my hand. When he opened his mouth to speak, he began choking. I slapped him. When things weren't all right, I got down on my knees to level with him, my face towards his. That's when I noticed the curly white, I reached into his mouth and began to yank, a telephone cord begat a telephone. Kid fell over once I pulled the entire receiver out of his jaw. Peter was on the other end of the line.

Hi Zach, how are you today. I'm doing fine Peter how did you know to reach me here? I'm in the woods too, dummy. We just wanted to know when you're driving us out of here. Peter I just unearthed a most fascinating archeological relic, please tell the others to come hither before it fades. This is not an appropriate time for fornicating an era, Peter replied sternly. But it's not…It is a burnt rectitude clearly giving off a vibrato aura. None of us deserve it. The child suddenly woke up.

I thought you were dead, I told it. The child could no longer speak. The phone cord had mangled his voice box. He still had his fingers though, at least two of them, that much was clear. With them, he pointed in one direction, then the other. My forehead quivered. Stop that, I yodeled. Everything around me shaking. Lightning struck the middle of the triangle. The child, unmolested, was gone, my friends suddenly surround me.

We went looking for the old man. The old man who had a new name for everything surrounding. When we determined rightly he'd disappeared, we noticed you'd gone. So then we set out to find you. At that point, we had two people to find, so we knew the situation was lifeless, desperate. After all, this is a strange forest that none of us can afford. Taylor piped in his garrulous contribution, it wasn't enough for any of us to implement. But then Taylor had a vision beamed to him. He stopped about a kilometer away from forest cactus. There was nothing else on the forest floor, just a bunch of dirt and knives. He brushed them all aside. What was with this particular spot, we had to wait to find out. Taylor brushed aside all must and all sharpness to reveal a single electrical socket. How had that socket been installed in the middle of this nowhere we found ourselves invading. No way of knowing how we'd ever make our way back to the car. A deep window, vowel-like, carved in the middle of an oak tree. Within shat a midget reminder, staring out at our unrepresented forces. Taylor shushed us all when restlessness threatened to overtake our statuary. He removed a single brown leaf from the floor and slid it into the electrical socket so elegantly, I thought his shoes might fall off. A powerful lapidary force shriveled the earth beneath our birkenstocks and suddenly we were transported to this very spot here, next to you.

At home, before he lived with others, Adam would sometimes lock himself in the darkness of his closet in order to imitate the hum of fluorescent lighting.

Peter picked up a branch and started to scream at it. He was angry because he no longer wished to be outside. Peter calm down, Matthew protested, we knew in the beginning what we were committing ourselves towards when we agreed to journey forth in perpetuity. What boggles you now?

This force is not something that will lead to any amiable gratuity of reconciliation. I just want out of here, even if I have to go back to that creek and swim till I reach the waterfall.

What a joyfully splendid bargaining tool, Lukas suddenly ejaculated. But I do think this forest will be worth coming back to to commit suicide in.

We will do it when we have sufficient angularity, Zach interjected, not unangrily at all either. He had had his authority undermined at least twice on that watershed day, and wasn't about to let his authority appear naked under the leafless twilight.

On our way back to the car, the Whore jumped up out of a pile of dead leaves someone had buried her in, screaming her fucking face off. She picked up a rake and started beating Zach in the face with the handle. Adam grabbed her and stuck her head in the dirt. You want me to kill her, Zach? Should I kill the bitch?

Let her live, Taylor spat out from afar. Everyone turned to look at him. He cast a gray shadow protruding in seven directions all at once. Trust me, he said, her constant annoying interjections will come to comprise a formative aspect of our collective legacy.

At that, we let her go off in silence. A moose chased after her. Peter, tears streaming down his face, began to sing.

No one knows what love is really all about. That's why there are so many songs in this world. God designed the animals to keep watch over us. People always do the wrong things. There are so many reasons why this world does not belong to us, it makes me tired to name them. But one only has one chance in every narrative. Adam lifts his shirt up to reveal two synthetic nipples. Taylor put goggles on before he drove us out of there.

Oh the children in the forecast, how it hurts me so. From the highway, I could see the shadow of the little boy who had helped me back at the stream. The child that the philosopher had become, before both disappeared in the forest's valiant act of magnetism. I brought some of the things back to hide, but others must remain there. If we were to import the entire forest back to our homeland, the vocabulary of the natives would falter. As such, there is no need to be tender with the highway. Turn on the air conditioning and blast my soul back to Mexico.

What do we want to listen to, Lukas mumbled from the front seat. No music is good enough for this moment, Zach responded, a lightweight scent of iron on his breath. Zach is right, said Adam, I don't want to be confused anymore. The only time confusion is allowed to subside is when you're in your mother's breasts, someone said. Shut up I shouted as Peter hung outside the windowsill.

A trucker blew past us, waving with no teeth. His windows stained blue from the smoke of hopelessness, I wondered aloud if he had a pet snake. We jammed our car inside the silence, and a gas station with no mailbox materialized on the highway. The attendant looked like some famous movie star I had no desire to meet. A few miles away, our suicide satellite crashed into the sign of a garden supply shop. The owner ran outside, cursing the almighty. But the almighty was too busy pissing on a fire hydrant to notice.

A wasp terrorized Adam's spider. Don't get all buttholish on me Zach Feral I am not the sort of self you can preserve. Lukas and Zach were having an argument in the front seat. You couldn't blame them for trying (to communicate). All other vespers were dead inside that vehicle. Gas station attendant came out to give us our receipt. Hey, weren't you the ones in that movie?

CHAPTER 8

Back on the highway leading to the
other america.
The Suiciders
captured by men in fur coats!
Taylor's
satanic flashback.
A witch turns them all into hairs.

The last guy I fucked was so lousy in bed I wanted to punish him when it was over. That motherly instinct pops up in me whenever I consider things that matter. I look up the light in the doorway where Jesus H. is standing. She makes parrot motions. Smell my armpits and begin to cry. I know the floor is my friend.

I don't want to wait at this highway reststop lounge for the rest of my existence (there isn't much left?). Shadows of glands are all around me. Teenage scientist comes in to take my temperature. There are so many stories similar to this one.

It should be flowing now that you're out of things to say. Fat City owner sent us in the wrong damn direction. We don't want to go back now, it would mean re-writing the entire story. We've come too far for that.

The philosopher of language yelled at me. Jesus is there for us even when we don't need her. She gets in the way like that. We should kill her. No, says Adam, she's my goddamn pet, the only thing I have in this lifestyle besides my boner. Shut the fuck up, Adam. We're just some teenage kids with bad hair and no disease. In order to get pure, we must cleanse our speech of all indiscretions, then drop a carpet bomb.

Old car wasn't good enough, so we had to steal a new one. Our legacy had grown to include more people—namely Taylor. I say namely even though I was never sure of his name. Lukas can't be my friend anymore and that's what stalls us. Adam's boner stabs my left temple. The schoolbus ahead of us on the highway made me realize that there were beings younger than us on this continent. The information is never available.

There was a wedding taking place in the cemetery. We crept past, careful to make our presence unfelt. A ferret bit Zach on the ankle, a curse as loud as a whisper. We faced the chain-link fence and hoped the other end would be dogless. All we wanted was freedom from imbecility and roaches, and that freedom would come in the form of a four-wheel drive.

To avoid the spokes, we tossed a blanket on top. Zach was gonna climb first; he wanted to prove something. I don't know what it was, the freedom? Before he had a chance to finish the climb, however, we found ourselves surrounded by men in white fur coats. One shone a flashlight directly on to Jesus H.'s delightful featherage; merak, merak! he barked at them ferretfully.

This syndrome does not require a diagnosis, spoke the centrifugal fur coat man, whose eyes weren't awash in silence. As soon as your foot hits the other side of that fence, an alarm will go off that will cause the ground to quake. We've been watching you Suiciders for some time now. Yours is a force that is easy to prognosticate.

They've been following us? Adam asked his parrot, confused. The dollop was something like mega. In his pants, I thought I saw another reality. But when I undid the zipper, all I found was yet another form of rage.

Fur coat flew his flashlight in our general direction; it landed in Peter's wig. The way one holds oneself can match one definition of lightness. He did a swift kick and flashlightman went flying out of his fur coat. Jesus flew down and severed his sidekick's jugular. Zach jumped over the fence and the goddamn ground shook. He had to get a car fast so we could escape the earthquake that would soon cause the entire region to sink into the great lake of moral fiber. To be a motherfucker in this environment is to bake cakes with the girl scouts while secretly threatening to employ them. Like all the others, Adam was torn between duty and salvation.

Get in the car stop standing there and reciting a list of your deficiencies. I'm sorry Zach I didn't know you were ready to goddamn rescue me yet is that okay? Some days I can't do anything but think. Stay up all night and defend yourself through the silence. Trembly void stinks like the dead squirrel we stuck on new car's antenna as identificatory measure.

A witch came and turned us all into tiny hairs with the pure power of her mind. Peter became a blonde hair; Zach was a curly red hair; Lukas was a black pube, thin as a wire; Adam was a sparkle hair; Matthew was an afro hair; Jesus was a brown hair. Even though Zach was a hair, he could still drive the car. The Sex Change Chorus came and sang us an instructional manual on how to function in our new guise. There are putrid objects out there that even I don't want to know anything about. Who are you singing to and how many words mark out your freedom. We were always going somewhere in those years.

There was one fur coat man who couldn't be killed, however, and this is the one who shot Lukas. That's how we ended up going to Fat City and getting misdirected. Here comes a thin blade of understanding. You can't go in the grass once you've become a hair. The grass becomes a forest, and then you wind up getting lost, just like we did earlier. Who knows, perhaps at that point we had already become hairs and had merely forgotten about it. Such stealthy ambivalence is always fully loaded with the force of untrammeled cliché. Zach's projected self-image was threatening to destroy us all. We couldn't question his stance as Leader, we didn't want to. Thankfully Taylor was there to balance that equation. His was a silence that reigned fully loaded over Zach's squelched malfeasance. That's enough character assessment for now. The friends were united and ready for adventure.

We pulled over at a roadside motel, hoping to cause a riot. Taylor snuck in up the back staircase, set off all the fire alarms, then ran back outside. He hopped back into the car and sat on Adam's face. Step on the gas Peter we need to get out of here before motel security catches up with us.

I want you all to know that I did that for psychological reasons, said Taylor. Lukas picked up a microphone and put a condom on it. He just wanted to fucking say something. To put his face in the microwave and die. Peter is laughing for no goddamn reason. What are you laughing at Peter? I saw a toad back there. On the highway. It looked so funny, all squished and dead. Reminded me of my mother back at home. Then he cried. This isn't the right environment. Why is it always based on catastrophe, why.

The lesbian got run over. She had too many friends, we had to annihilate her. That Cher song everyone hates came on the radio, spurred a relapse in Adam. He started shrieking all womanly so loud it made my bowels churn and my cock squirt out the star spangled banner. Cherry-flavored rectum turned upside down. Adam get your faghag out of this car right now. But I'm not even gay. It doesn't matter, you don't have to be gay for the lovin to be so wrong.

A christmastree in her bra. The entertainers got killed. Let's go have a party.

Explain to us the psychological reason for setting off the motel fire alarm.

It's because I was abused. I didn't have a normal home life, you see. My father gave birth to me. Then he left me all alone to dwell with my mother in her cancer-ridden shack. Her breath was so bad, I almost died. She got a new man who turned me on to satan. They baptized me in a river of drool. Everyone in the whole goddamn town was involved, it was nuts, a nightmare.

Let's go eat us some fast food.

Peter: I need someone to live on top of me for the rest of my days. A view of a person's face can tell you a lot about their meaning.

After the dog raped me, mama's boyfriend come in to tell me something bout art. Art is something that vibrates when you throw up on it. Zach it comes time to tell your story. No Lukas has a story to tell as well. I want to hear Peter's. He started but wasn't able to finish. Taylor's the one who got traumatized and learned a sorry lesson. There are no nouns.

Once I was able to escape the clutches of the satanic cult, I realized religion wasn't for me. That's when I began to believe in the things I could see. Before, I kind of doubted they were really there. I figured it was all just a ginormous illusion put here to confuse me into loving myself.

Lukas's first sexual experience was a VHS cassette tape. His dad told him he was old enough to learn something. He came in and gave him that tape, told him never let your mama see it. He waited till his dad and mom had gone off to the grocery store to buy them a new son, then slipped it in the player. He saw a big fat man with a gorilla mask on fucking his mom. There's no violence there. There's no there there either.

Realism gives me a headache. I'm way too confused to be listening to you right now let me out of this car. As part of a ritual, we made Lukas's girlfriend bake her afterbirth in a pie, which we then dropped off at the local army recruiter's office. Hey, Matthew suddenly interrupted, there are coins down here all over the floor mats! Woo-hoo! (We almost forgot that Matthew had a story too.) There are so many soap opera stars I want to find out about.

Your personal life bores me, Matthew. Clean up all the coins, we're going to get some fast food.

I like my food cooked slow. Replace the coins with spools of yarn. They feel so much better to put your feet on when you are on a long ass car ride with sparks behind you. Lukas just said he wants to go back to the forest. But we don't follow his rules. This isn't a game that a teenage loser can play. If you don't know what's for sale, then don't try and cook the vegetables.

What is Adam's story?

You didn't let me get to my point yet, Taylor says, tears filling his eyes. I'm sorry, I didn't know there was one. That man in the fur coat back there, the one who shot Lukas—that was my father once.

That fur coat fool? Not the owner of Fat City? I thought he was your rightful father.

No, I'm sorry, you don't understand me. I meant the fur coat he was wearing—that white fur coat used to be my father.

How could a white fur coat be your father; I thought he belonged to a satanic cult?

It was that witch who's been following us. She's the one remnant of the town I can't escape. That place of my childbirth. I mean the place that I grew up on, me a cancerous growth in all my weightlessness. The same witch who turned us all into hairs she turned my father into a fur coat. We need to go back there so I can finally reconcile my mediocrity to his fate. Otherwise the curse will never be lifted, that witch will be upon us until the hour of our drowning, we will forever be fine hairs in the thinness of this whirl.

At the rest stop, I went into the bathroom to find Adam dying his hair blonde in the sink. I grabbed him and shoved his face in the toilet; flushed. Adam was moaning and squeaking. I told him never to dye his hair blonde without asking my permission first.

…Then I felt a sharp, stabbing pain in my bowels. I couldn't help it; I let out a sort of yelp. The pain spread to my groin area, then I felt something moving through my anus. The head of a serpent made its way on to the floor through my ass. They had somehow fit an entire snake up there, and with the help of a mirror that they'd set in front of my ass, I was able to watch the whole thing as though it were happening on TV. Despite the pain, I was reminded of a magic trick I once saw at a carnival. I could still taste the shit mother had put in my mouth earlier. Now she bent down, cupping the snake in the palms of her hands. Then she grabbed it, its tail whipping around back and forth, and bit its head off. The snake's tail kept squirming around even after its head was torn off. Like a post-death reflex. Like it didn't really want to be dead. They removed the bolts from my feet and dragged me by the arms over to a candlelit altar. Robert was there. Robert—that was the name of mom's boyfriend, the black wizard. Before he turned white and became a fur. He had a mean expression on his face. It scared me. I hadn't known that side of him before. A metal operating table was wheeled out. Like the kind of stretcher they use to take people to the emergency room. There was a little baby on it. The baby was crying. The chanting rose in volume as the hysterical baby's cries echoed throughout the chamber. Mother lifted the baby off the stretcher, put it on the altar in front of Robert. He picked up an instrument—what looked like a scalpel, I guess—and proceeded to slash through the baby's center in a very deliberate, methodical fashion. I started crying really soft—the tears running down my face. Blood from the baby squirted on to me. The masked figures—they were dancing all around. I was forced to stand there and watch it all transpire. Robert removed the baby's heart and intestines. I'm not sure if it was my little brother, where they got the baby from. He passed the organs to my mother. She stood over me and let the entrails rain down through her fingers. Then she dug her hands into the baby's corpse like she was cleansing them, then wiped them all over my naked body. I was shaking all over. Flashes of white light in a room shaped like a circle—no corners to hide in…

Shut the fuck up Taylor you're making all this up.

That's what TV Talk Show Hostess said too. You've gotta be better than her, or else I can't continue onwards.

What's taking them so long are they drowning in the goddamn toilet.

Close.

Adam came out with blonde hair, Zach pointing a knife at him. See this faggot? See what he done goddamn did? Any of you motherfuckers tries to turn blonde on me, I'll gouge your eyes out.

We were silent for a few hours, just the roar of an occasional truck passing us by. I think the silence was put there on purpose, it was meant to define us. Some higher entity.

We arrived at the witch doctor's house at high noon. It was Taylor who led us there; just like he knew who the witch was, he knew where we had to go to get rid of the witch. I was perplexed to find that the witch doctor was a teenager just like us. Since he didn't have blonde hair, I considered for a moment asking him to join our band. I was already thinking of a replacement for Adam. He was housed in a cherry-flavored gazette on a service road off the highway. As soon as we entered his lair, I could smell the reverence that pervaded the air. Some narrow fool playing guitar in the other room. Kill the fish to snare the shark.

So you came here to get rid of the hag that was following you.

We went to pre-school together, said Taylor, maybe you remember.

The witch doctor nodded to his gymnastic mistress; she somersaulted out of the room.

In order for me to kill the witch and restore you all to your pre-hair state, you must listen to the story I tell you. This mere act of listening will bore you into a hypnotic tunnel. This witch, she will follow you there, and we will trap her with our surprise ending—an ending which elicits an actual form of endlessness that certainly you must all relate to:

CHAPTER 9

What the witch doctor says

W e were at the dollar store when a leopard-skinned man snatched Grandma's purse. Her eyes changed from blue to green, but she didn't bother chasing him down. We could've easily overtaken him—there were twenty-two of us. We waited for Grandma to give the command, but nothing came. The shop attendant was attending to something else, no strip mall security in sight. No one dared move; we just waited. When Grandma determined it was time, we followed her out into the parking lot, where the churchmobile took up two handicap spaces.

Back at the Cold Blood Ranch, the Cherry twins were using the intestines of a freshly slaughtered hog for jump rope. Their rhymes were all about Truth and the legacy of boredom one must submit to in order to get there.

Now I'm not what you'd call a born follower, and neither is my little brother Samuel. Samuel was just twelve when we left our home for Cold Blood. We'd first discovered Grandma on the

Power Station one night round 2am, waiting for Mama to get home from the sausage factory that employed her at the time. She was surrounded by a group of her followers—must have been about a dozen of them. Her rainbow mohawk glittered under the lights of the Cold Blood televisual command unit. What impressed me most was the seeming lack of a program. They weren't trying to sell us Jesus like all the other midnight preachers. Grandma preferred to hum her message, staring straight ahead. It may sound funny, but there was something mesmerizing about the way she held herself there. Samuel started laughing, asking what the hell is this, but it was my turn with the remote control that night, and besides, there was nothing else on at that hour.

What is unnamable is often true. The next time we saw them, we knew it was a real thing—not just some TV gag. About sixteen of them standing around the churchmobile in the parking lot of the coliseum. I was so horny, I had been sniffing glue in the backseat of someone's car, I climbed out to look for a wooded area where I could puke and jerk off. The sight of them stopped me from going any further. They all looked the same—the white cloth, the angelic faces, the mohawks. I didn't know what to say or do, I didn't know if it was just the glue or if this was somehow real, I didn't immediately connect them to the broadcast we'd witnessed a few years prior. I heard Samuel's voice call my name. Iron Maiden would be going on soon. They knew I was looking, but I tried to walk past them anyway.

I don't know how, but they got me into the churchmobile. Grandma was in there. It was all but empty, save for an orange light and a T-shaped beam, human-size, made out of wood. I remember them handcuffing me to each side of the horizontal slab. I was quivering, but still high. I couldn't protest, anyway.

Grandma had taken full control of my psyche. It's like I was stunned. I didn't even whimper when they tightened the noose around my neck. A flash went off in front of me. Grandma waved a Polaroid photo in front of my face so I could see how I looked. Then Grandma's yellow mouth was right in front of my eyeballs. You see that? she asked in a throaty whisper. That's exactly how Christ looked right before he croaked.

The Christian version of God was invented to poison our minds and put us on the path of false salvation—a concept that is synonymous with self-destruction. Grandma is there to correct all that. There is such a thing as death, but there are also ways to go on living even beyond the *apparent* state of death. The vast majority of us, however, have not been made aware of this. Death as a science has not been properly investigated, because the version of science that is currently practiced on our planet is insufficient. You have to go beyond those simplified formulae to find out the truth. Take Grandma, for instance. She has died at least five times on the human level, and yet she goes on living. Even when we die in the current sphere of life, there is a way that we may go on. But it's not so simple. You have to watch Grandma, learn from her, to figure out how.

It's not what you think. They're real nice people, a lot more human than most you meet. That's our whole purpose: to become thoroughly human, in a transcendent sense. Once you figure this out, you will see that it is the only path in life that really makes sense.

Now, what you have to understand is that there are two types of dogs: left-brained dog and right-brained dogs. Only Grandma can tell, through its behavior, what type of dog is which. The right-brained dogs are just filthy animals and should be ignored—they have no genuine purpose. A small minority of the dog population, however, is left-brained. Left-brained dogs contain messages that, when interpreted correctly, teach us things about death and how to go beyond it.

In a way, everything clicked into place. By that time, Mom had already exited the picture. She wound up getting swept off her feet by the owner of the sausage factory, never had time for me and Samuel. She became a celebrity of sorts, the spokeswoman for the american sausage industry. The only time we ever saw her was on TV talk shows. Grandma offered us a new home at the Cold Blood Ranch and a whole new way of being.

It took Samuel a lot longer to adjust. Him being younger, it was harder to instill the new mind in him that was needed. I'd wake up in the middle of the night, go into the bathroom, find Samuel in there talking to the toilet. The others thought it might help for Samuel to take on more responsibility, feel himself a part of the nucleus. So the preparation of the left-brains became his duty.

Grandma likes them prepared in a certain way. You take it out of the Tupperware and put it straight on the microwave disk. Power level 10, five-and-a-half minutes. This usually softens it up enough to mash with a fork. Meanwhile, you bring a can of Campbell's chicken rice soup to boil, mix it in the brains, and it's ready for Grandma to ingest.

One day, Samuel fell into one of his lapses in the middle of the process. I walked in to find him standing in front of the microwave, an empty expression. The dog brain had exploded from the heat, splattered all over the glass, while the plate continued to spin round and round before Samuel's empty eyes.

I took him back to our sleep cell, shut the door. Thankfully, the others were off hunting frogs. He was completely morose, yet sweaty, so I peeled off his cloth and lay down next to him on the cot we shared. I don't know how long we were there, but I must've dozed off, because when I woke up, Grandma was standing above me. Where's my brain? she croaked. I feel another revelation coming on.

Samuel wasn't there, but the whole room smelled like his breath, so he couldn't have been gone for very long.

You weren't really supposed to do anything most of the time. If you needed to be transported, that's what the frogs were there for. Carrier frogs is what she called them. While they're still alive, you put their behind in your mouth and wait for the journey to arrive. It was a way of traveling that wasn't physical. Still, you go places. Grandma's always with you, though. Afterwards, you're supposed to report back to her. Once a frog has been used in this fashion, you kill it, then remove the skin. The skin can be smoked or consumed, and you have a similar experience.

We couldn't find Samuel after the incident with the exploded brains. He was gone for three days, three days in frog time, maybe longer in the human sphere. We checked everywhere, but no one on the ranch had seen anything.

I was getting desperate. I was starting to feel things I hadn't for ages—human emotions. It wasn't pleasant. I knew that it was steering me off course. If I was going to do this, what I had been chosen to do—overcome death in all its forms and graduate to the next sphere—I needed Samuel by my side.

I requested permission to leave the ranch for a few hours. Grandma would never allow us to leave on our own, but she didn't feel like going herself, so she sent Cousin Spidertoe along so that we could monitor one another while away from the ranch.

We found Samuel in a field not far making love to a cow. A few months later, there would be human babies with cowheads sucking on Milkweed's udders in that very same field.

Back at the ranch, Grandma was in the kitchen. A fresh batch of frogs could be heard croaking in the fridge. She just looked at Samuel, didn't say anything. As if by looking, she already knew all there was to say. Grandma didn't have a lot of patience with talkers. She taught us to minimize that form of communication in favor of other, more extrasensory ones.

All virgins are perverts, but not all perverts are virgins. This was Grandma's response when I told her that I was worried about Samuel. I'm going to send you on a mission—alone, she said. But you can't tell anyone about it.

I had known about Grandma's special powers for some time, but had yet to witness an actual miracle. Now she was entrusting me with a mission: to gather the fodder necessary for the spell. The spell that would rescue my brother from the nympho-demons.

The holes in the sky are called stars in the human language. I laid in my sleeping bag in the middle of the desert, staring up at them. In a way, I reflected, it all went back to Mama. Her selfish erotic behavior. Not that she had ever molested me or Samuel. It's just that she made it clear from the first day that one part of a man's anatomy would always mean more to her than either one of us. Samuel was doing his best to compensate, now that he was old enough to come to that realization. He just couldn't see that he was destroying both of us via those cravings he wasn't making a strong enough effort to contain.

As I drifted off to sleep, I composed a letter to Mama in my head.

Dear Mama,

Maybe your life is an illusion. Maybe you really killed yourself in the middle of it and then forgot in order to go on living like the big fat radiator you are. Cos you give off heat but don't get anything in return. I know that you're secretly still alive somewhere out there in that big bad wolf of a world. I saw you on the TV screen once being interviewed by that celebrity sausage grinder, whatsername. You had a string hanging off of your head with a rat tied to the end of it and no politics. I got shipped off to Grandma's ranch to learn how to be a man in this world. I'm through with the learning, Mama. I remember Dad telling me that whenever he put his thing inside you, it felt like there was a tin ashtray between your legs. I know you wanna grow up and become a child just like me, but you'll never learn the ways of this world like I have. And the idea of having to baptize you in such a shallow river of drool makes me lunge for that filthy bar of soap we share for our communal midnight scrubbings. I love Grandma now, and I'm only allowed to love one of you at a time, let alone wait around until your inner child kills himself.

Love,

Samuel

who is not your real son

The next morning, I felt happy to be alive for once. Grandma says we die a little bit each time we go to sleep, the dreams we have are records of that particular instance of dying. That day, I found all the things I needed: a dead copperhead, some hawk eyes, three arrows. The leader of the tribe gave me a bag of salt which, being pale and greedy, I consumed before my return. I picked the most poisonous flower I could find and painted a picture of Grandma's face on it. I drove an antique car out of nowhere. I followed her directions, and I followed them well.

When I got back to the shack, Samuel was strapped to a rack. Grandma was there, purple smoke pouring out of her mouth. This spell is going to make Samuel stop getting erections, she explained to the others. Samuel's eyeballs were bulging. What time is it? Grandma asked. Samuel had curlers in his hair. He was naked, his penis stood up like a soldier, steam bled from his frightened skin. I wanted to tell him everything I knew, that everything was going to be okay, that Grandma would fix all the broken parts. But I knew that it wouldn't be until after the operation that he'd be able to understand our language. If he had been able to talk at that moment, I'm sure he would have repented, asked us to spare him the procedure. As Grandma cut into him with the first arrow, I focused on the sound of the frogs croaking, which you could hear if you tried hard enough. The croaks and the way they fed into the hum of the refrigerator, and pretty soon, all was fog in my field of perception.

That night, Samuel and I shared a cot in the sleep cell. We were all alone, as the others had been instructed to sleep in a different location. It was just us and Grandma at the ranch. In the middle of the night, a terrible hacking sound roused me. Samuel was still exhausted from the spell, so he was able to sleep through it all. Grandma was having a coughing fit in her cell, but it went on for so long and sounded so awful that I was eventually persuaded to go check on her.

I stood outside the cell, calling her name. No one was allowed to enter, of course, except occasionally another female. I stood there calling out to Grandma, but the horrible sound continued, oblivious to my pleas. I couldn't stand it any longer. I pushed the door open.

The hacking. It came not from Grandma, but what she had been turned into. Whether or not she had willed this herself—if this was the next life for her and she'd known it all along and just not said anything about it to anyone—or the erection spell that she had cast on Samuel had gone terribly awry, the fact is that where I expected to find Grandma, I instead found a giant toad, about the size of a man's shoe.

Suddenly Samuel was standing there beside me. He blinked his eyes, dazed. The hacking came every time the toad stuck out its tongue. Grandma? Is that you? There was no other possibility. Yes, Samuel answered on the thing's behalf. That's her.

We were afraid, afraid for Grandma, so we took her into our cell to sleep with us. She looked so vulnerable, hacking and ribbiting all alone in there. We felt the need to protect her in her new cold blooded guise.

A single silver ray shot through a crack in the curtains, bringing us into the new day. I was there before Samuel. I sat up in the cot, trying to get my bearings. Then Samuel startled me by letting out a tremendous scream. I looked down. Samuel's penis, it was soft, but it had grown so much while he was asleep that it now ran down the entire length of his leg. As I studied its trail to the other side of the mattress, I found that it culminated in a bloody green mess, a blob of gore on Samuel's left foot.

Sleep brings lots of commotion with it. Me and Samuel, we've always both been big kickers, so it's never a good idea to sleep together. But being brothers, we've grown used to all the bruises and toenail stabbings over the years, and don't mind it so much. That's why we didn't give it much thought when we brought

Grandma to sleep with us. I don't know who squished her that night—whether it was me or Samuel, or whether our unconscious bodies had collaborated in a particularly consuming nightmare.

If there's one lesson we learned from Grandma, it's resourcefulness in the face of death. Or so-called death. And I had already made up my mind, having been reborn countless times, what it meant to live forever. I didn't panic. I just went straight to the refrigerator, opened the door, and picked me out another Grandma. This one ribbited loudly and pissed in my hand as I picked her up.

I took Grandma into the drawing room, opened the curtains. There's a white wall right in front of the window. I've spent entire days just sitting there, staring at it.

Samuel came in with an emotional expression on his face that I couldn't decipher. My penis, he exclaimed, I think the nympho-demons are attacking it again.

Go do something about it, fool. Don't talk about it here in front of Grandma.

Samuel ran off, I sat down in front of the great white wall. Grandma leaped onto my right leg. I considered licking her, but then thought better of it. Instead, I conjured up a best friend, who came and sat down with us. Me and Grandma started to tell him the whole story, from beginning to end. We didn't have a lot of time; the others would be back before nightfall. Not far away, you could hear a woman or a small child screaming. In the driveway, the Cherry twins used a string of pig hearts for jump rope and sang their broken song:

> *witch's brew*
> *tastes like spew*
> *three fat frogs*
> *with nothing to do*

CHAPTER 10

Florida:

an allegory.

No longer hairs, we had to keep moving, paranoid they would catch us, whoever *they* might be in this particular instance: the midget porn star alliance, the men in fur coats, the police, the motorcycle men, the witch, someone's parents, or some even more nefarious force yet to be burdened with a name. Taylor suggested we hide out at his cousin's down in FL.

By the time we got to Kelli's house, we were all blonde. Kelli—Taylor stood in the front yard screaming—don't you want to come outside and play with sacred member. You don't have to worry about the witches in the alleyway no more, we've been cured.

Kelli hadn't left her house in 13.4 years. We were the only tyrants left in that country of ours.

Post-apocalyptic brainfuck swinging on the front porch. Kelli came out in her bathrobe to confront our blondeness. She decided to sing a song that she didn't know the words to.

Kelli was a former soap opera star who offered no forgiveness. As a woman she had so much to live for. As a man she had nothing to do.

Shove a butterfly up yr ass Lukas we can't slipstream the vibration before the cosmos get all farty. My blonde army would take no direction. We went inside the house to get another view of the front porch.

There were no projections on the walls, I had to get out of there. My foot fed the silence rightfully. Taylor brought out the Jew's harp and made a goddamn hootenanny unfurl. With blonde hair, Adam had become a Mexican.

Smell my armpits and begin to cry. I know the floor is my friend.

The floor was Kelli's best friend. Whenever she puked, she would make a squealing noise that would invariably awaken Matthew and Arnold from whatever coma they had drifted into on that particular evening.

We just relapsed in the narrative structure back into a preordained gyration, dictated by principles of voice. Zach's laughter threatened to drown out the discourse in the kitchen. Taylor was trying to convince soap star cousin Kelli to be a refuge for the gang's lawlessness. Kelli couldn't agree; she had her career to think about.

Get that bad perm away from this logic. I've worked so hard to get me this here house in Florida, I ain't gonna let some unknown debauchery take that all away from me.

Peacefulness is never enough to have once cared about, Kelli. I think you're losing your grip on the reality TV.

I don't want to be raped in a satisfactualized context, she whispered through her teeth at him. Adam and Lukas were in the living room dropping acid. Zach wandered in and pissed inside the VCR. Shrimpless wayfare signatory device.

Once we had Kelli tied up in the bedroom, Taylor brought out the category placement machine. A flavorful eruption instead. Groved features endowed us with plenty of mysticism to unravel as our hair dried in the oven.

Adam was frustrated. I want to be as terrible as you one day, he told Zach. The fire hydrant outside of Kelli's house was filled with cough syrup. They decided to go on a neighborhood tricycle ride.

Too many motherfuckers in this house, the soap star called out from her bedroom. Get em out get em out get em out.

We're not leaving until the police has disappeared, Taylor grunted back in her general direction. This world was built for fear, and we're the criminals in it? A new world disaster area is what I crave. Anything to heal the wounds inflicted on my marginal existence by the sham of secrecy. You were in on it too, Kelli, I can recognize by your gesture. TV cameras came inside the house to re-arrange our chronology of defeats. Reality: a goldfish musical. We've gotta present our message to the people somehow.

Zach picked up an acoustic guitar and began to strum up some revolutionary momentum.

I hate this current brand of satisfaction. If that bitch don't shut up we're gonna have to go back into that bedroom and get us another job application. I know what you mean outside the sunny window?

Holiday faggots all filled to the brim with barfola. Mustache mistake! The name a form of higher righteousness. It gets hard to emphasize your thoughts outside the trampoline. Mom's a high carriage, her horse fell on the electric piano. One problem is there are too many visions in a single paragraph. I'm fat now.

My grandma is a man. Go back to the former paradise. It's hard to find something out these days.

The artist must now live in a state of perpetual distraction. Art will be the measure of response to those distractions.

Adam busied himself with an anteater coloring book. Dead witchcraft warrior appears to anomalize my routine. I shafted in to blubberless ambition before a moldy coffee tray smashed the ceiling-state. Take a picture of me serving my country; I survived the landfill.

Zach and Lukas were best friends. They constantly ate ice cream together. A charming warlord came over to make out with them. Lukas and Adam were best friends.

They're killing babies out there in the aftermath. You don't believe me. Well go to hell, bubble man.

Is it pointless to have a cat called Nigger in the 24th century, or will it all fade away, time, as utopia farts in my mouth? This is a question Kelli the soap star struggled with as she lay there all tied up. Some people just won't let the silence wrap their brains up. A collusion of simple words is enough to birth grief.

Kelli was such a fat bitch, she even ate when she weren't hungry. Style is a deathtone; call the police. The police is gonna come and take you away, to live in the land of no regards.

Kelli ran full slate ahead into the other america. She had to take a bath. Do you think Kelli looks like the Whore? Taylor said. I think there are other stars we should focus on destroying, said Adam, who was now wearing a hairnet.

Lukas do you want to go salsa-dancing with me tomorrow night.

My favorite faggot is a woman, Arnold replied. Some combination of both, to be militantly honest with you.

Kelli turned on the TV so that fat black bitch could tell her how to live her goddamn life in the here and now. There were no TV cameras watching as she watched TV. Thus, she had no reason to live anymore. That's when we showed up on her front doorstep looking to cross wires.

We couldn't get Adam to stop biting himself. He wanted the military to come and rescue him. This would be impossible, given the circumstances of our detachment. Exile is a cruel place for a world. Things to get excited about and things to run away from, sometimes one and the same. Purple van pulls up outside Kelli's house. Through the blinds, Zach describes the imperialist getting out on the driver's side. He shouts back at Matthew to hide the cocaine. Peter has a salmonella mustache. Some people are earless all the same.

I did something to myself that warranted an explanation. The cops out back ate caviar and discussed the score from last night's game. We ran away from the homeless ones who were chasing us. We had a mission to fulfill. Jesus screeched in the papaya tree. A certain deranged lesson to learn would keep us fit from merciful invaders who had no posture for our understanding. When are we going to the goddamn zoo?

Peter's father came over to put him in a movie. Peter didn't want to go. He had his friends to live for, he didn't need a career. Certain others had salt on them. The fish found out what you sat on my face for.

You have to feel sorry for Kelli. She feels uncomfortable as a human. She tried to eat her father's cock off in Hawaii. Pieces of pizza lodged in the sand.

The homeless people searched for their teeth in Kelli's front lawn. When the lights inside the plants turned on, I thought I was seeing a UFO. That's just how the neighbors communicate with each other, Kelli explained to us, a sock in her mouth. Lick my eyeball lick my eyeball—that was Adam shouting. He couldn't get off the chair, he was rolling around smoothly, his feet had become tacos. Lick my eyeball lick my eye. Adam I liked you better when you just squeaked.

Are we done hiding out yet, Matthew's complaining. Just send him Arnold, everyone needs a sacrifice now and then. But Arnold has no eyebrows, he can't witness the computer.

Lick my eyeball lick my eyeball lick my—

Lukas finally got sick of hearing it, stuck a screwdriver in Adam's socket and wrenched the eyeball right out. It fell on the floor, landing in a taco shell. Lukas squashed it under his foot. Eyeball juices landed on the cat and the electrical socket, causing the lights to do a flashdance.

I dedicate this number to your grief.

Zach, Lukas tore my fucking eye out.

Lukas was punished for his blonde acts. He was made to go into the bathroom and handwash all the hand towels. Peter and Matthew, meanwhile, manufactured a digital eye. They would give it to Adam on his twenty-third birthday, after he was already dead.

A steamy lubricant, this is my righteous pillow. We've got a woman tied up in the back bedroom, if you know what that looks like. We had to do it because the goddamn bitch doesn't know how to ruin her own career. She called Taylor's mom and told on us and now we've got the police, an army of midget porn stars, and a satanic cult on our trail. It's bad enough with the bikers, who started out our enemies and became our friends once Fat City worked its magical relapse into their addled cellulars. Now we've got a joint ambition train to crash before the lord of lawlessness catches up with us to make an announcement.

I don't have a problem with you calling my name, I just have a problem with knowing you. When you say she-male, I know you really mean Bulgaria.

Quit pretending like you know who I'm not, Adam, we've all been eyeless up to a certain point. When you say you're sorry, are you really looking out the window? Fuck local asses on your teenage computer stream!

Matthew was an amateur webcam. He wanted all his friends to see. Taylor went into the back bedroom to have a word with his tied-up cousin. Adam went to search for a new eyeball.

Taylor gagged Cousin Kelli the soap star with a day-old sock and slashed her throat. It was time to go on vacation. (Or at least the zoo!)

CHAPTER 11

Dreamdriving to the
other america.
The Suiciders
stop to shoot a
music video for the
digital age.

The boys were in the car dreaming. They had left Kelli's house at a quarter till eight.

They were upset because Taylor's mother was out to get them all. It was all because she called up Kelli and Kelli told her they were there. Now they had to elect a new leader because Zach didn't want to lead them anymore, he felt they weren't ready for suicide. A ten-inch reminder crept inside the vehicle when they were all asleep. There were membranes, all right, but there was also a lot of wood. Matthew don't drive this car when you're stupid. We need an axe to finish proposing her.

The Whore jumped on top of the windshield, gave them all instant hangovers. Is that scent what I think it is?

Oh, so now you've come to save us, is that it?

Get out of the car, Lukas.

Lukas stepped out in the middle of the highway and immediately began to play his bass. Traffic stopped and two sun-drenched vehicles got married.

Sometimes, at the root of exhaustion, we find something worth preserving.

I can't believe the elected official wishes to speak with us. It must mean we got a TV movie of the week.

The teenager came over and said something intelligent. Here come the invaders...

The invader got eaten out. You remind me of someone. I ate peanuts and thought about god. Lukas just crashed the car into a dry cleaner's. An evil stereotype comes out of the cash register to give us a moral reminder. You have blood on your teeth and it smells.

Adam, your cocksucking apparition of a father just called. He wants you to take the toilet out of the safe deposit box. He no longer needs you involved with his legacy.

I think it's because he appeared on nationwide television. Aren't you polite?

The asian just ran off with my lunch ticket. She needs you in the zoo.

There's something to be done about holding on to silence. We believe you when you claim to be a cherry device.

I was playing this game with Zach where I would be pretending to think about him whenever he looked over at me. It got on his nerves so much, he started to play the game back. Pretty soon we were all involved. Then the Whore drove a moped over Adam's face. When he got back up, he was no longer blonde, so he was allowed to rejoin the band. I was feeling scared when the choreographer came to prepare us for our music video shoot.

The asian got angry. He said that we couldn't shoot a music video when we had just wrecked our car in his dry cleaning service. So we gave him a tiny baby and told him he could do whatever he wanted with it, just as long as he didn't tell the cops. Then we were able to dance in front of the car wreck, people screaming at us all the while. Lukas did a backflip and landed on his abdomen. We were all there to mop up his spillage. The dry cleaner's tax accountant ran over and gave us all muffins. Once we finished dancing, we were able to look for a new car.

CHAPTER 12

Two cars, one highway.
An angel descends.
With the police hot on their trail,
the Suiciders get a room for the night
in a motel
with talking cats.
Adam the Cyclops writes.
Taylor takes charge. Or does he.

To be amused is always reckless, a dream. We were back in the car again. Suddenly I felt like singing. It came on too strong. Archipelago burgers need no salt. Arnold: Arnold's not there. He's unimportant, a visitor or too adolescent to be considered rough, all Matthew cares about is the roughness.

When Zach wants attention, he just stares out the window of his own spleen.

Taylor was gonna get us somewhere, and Zach was glad about that! Adam didn't want anymore holes in his remaining eyeball that night. He shouted out a forgiveness at Lukas for smashing his good eye. There were now two cars strapped together to traverse the abandoned highway. Loathing cell's bombastic nightblooms was the name of one, Sarah's teenage daughter was the other. Both cars contained friends. We were sniffing a revolution, there was no one ahead of us.

They were cracking down on us hard that year. We could feel them breathing down our necks, even when we couldn't otherwise see them. Time had trapped us in her royal clutch, the old cunt, and there was nothing we could do but laugh to dispel the symptoms of our own unease, a gesture that grew more futile with each execution.

We said fuck it one afternoon and took to the streets to protest something. No one remembers what, but it seemed necessary at the time. Important enough to endure the severe beatings of baton-wielding wingtipped ballerinas. Arnold claimed it was the police in disguise, as a particularly heavy-looking wand came crashing down on him. I'm sure he saw sparks before it all went black.

Here, eat this rat poison, said Zach. It will protect you against all pain.

But will it prolong the protest? Looks as though they got a handle on us.

Not one they know how to pull.

I opted for a mushroom instead. Then the police set fire to our fire and it was all over, before it even had a chance to end. Sort of like Vietnam.

I was still in the street when the juice kicked in. Suddenly it all made sense. I gathered the gang together, what was left of us, to plot the next move. Zach piped in once more.

I think there's too much disarray to make anything happen. It might be time to succumb. Announce defeat. Go our separate ways. Find a new crime...

Don't listen to this defector, Taylor interrupted. Taylor had something to live for. If we cease inventing visions to chase after, what's left? Utter randomness? How fulfilling is that? I elect we kill this joker and move on to the next vestibule. A new strata. There has to be something we haven't yet experienced. Let's hurry up and invent it before it finds us!

I second that emotion, shouted the one with the beard.

The van was parked over there, so I climbed in back to feed the mind machine. Making our way past the dancing bear, we stopped off at the mini-market for a shot at prime time.

Get me a bottle of suicide water, I ordered. Without gas.

Another fuel injection would keep me rolling for as long as it took. There had to be something left in this wasteland of broken entropy.

We were trying to figure out how to get through the road-block up ahead when an angel descended upon us. It wore a satin dress and a halo made of firecrackers.

Peace on earth and all that shit, it bellowed through its orifice. Before we get down to the truth, got any questions about the afterlife?

We exchanged glances, our glances seemed to know more than we did. The angel must have sensed this, because it proffered a desultory moan as though willing itself to recompense for our stalled insights. A sheet of lightning was hurled from the skies to make the cops disappear up ahead. I knew I'd be dead soon, and I didn't care. So much stimulation fatigues me, until I feel I can go no further. An imaginary line is drawn. It becomes a unit for measuring the despair of my trust in others, particularly those I willingly surround myself with. At the end of the line lies our mutual goal, a picture that becomes more blurred each time one of us, as an individual, looks in that direction. At the end of the day, it is best to ignore it altogether. We've managed that. If only what we are left with, the question of our collective self, could be so simple. I think the angel lingered in that spot for a while after we sped away, in pursuit of any answer.

We were there the night chip daniels died, someone could be heard saying in the next motel room.

Taylor turned on the evening news. We were hoping for a sign, to see ourselves out there and maybe not feel so naked once again. Adam and Lukas were doing something together in the bathroom (having sex? Don't be gay). A whole nation of vegetables calling out at us through the guise of the late night station.

Why can't you tell me who I am? You can't win the war, you're too blocked. My favorite reptile. Are you devoted to helping me or mutilating me? The term dictates the reason. Screw chronology. Fate has a booboo on its shin. Lukas tells me they discovered a new fish today called it a she. How can you know for sure a fish's genitalia, Taylor answered. These are all versions of somebody else's story I'm telling. It can't be that awry. People are lucky to not know me, always stick to the unbroken story, the one we can never be made of. Outside the snow has stopped snowing. Outside there is a world I will forever refuse to glorify. Outside it's dark, the rays of the world originate at the center of my brain. Let me tell you a story about light. It starts with this girl. This girl who thought she was a fish.

I demand action out of everyone I see, and thus: make something happen. Says Zach. The tropical highlights aren't there anymore, across this face. It was my plan to be blocked, a game of Hide and Tell. Object mystique is a patter causes floating. You are so superficial it is hard to tell, says Adam. Admit you don't know something when it sees you. Repetition creates illusion. Some were glad he was dead; for others, a mere case of blathering.

To be stumped is not object-friendly. Barely a week went by, the sky caused a new addiction.

Adam writes in his notebook. He knows all the words he wants in there. To write like your tongue is on fire. A ruinous masterpiece. Smashed fragments so nice to be sniffing you out love, it's like a paradox?

Reality is way too complicated. Even for those who manage to conquer it.

As Adam writes, Lukas lies on the same bed, studying the gnarly motel blanket. Maybe the blanket stands for vulnerability. Too many animals all over it.

Peter doesn't like the stench of old coffee. It is too late to spill oil all over the face of god who is shitting olives into a grape jar, full-on lava my excessive holiday—so much to bury, a rope pokes through the sand. You can pull your own way through it, you can advise them to remain seated and grown. A noise is admitted by the antlers, kids. You have grown satisfied with the selfish desires you ever once thought to contain. A magic fish in the ocean; soviet thoughts blackened by soft fears. Adam's testicles aren't plastic. We thought more of exile in those years than the bells ringing right outside our door. Climb the chimney to face god: smoke is ultimate, fear an invisible thread. Traumatize the banana before speaking to it.

I remember feeling so naked with myself whenever I went out when I was younger. I ate whatever life threw my way. When I bit something too hard to sorrow, I gave it away to whomever's mouth wide open enough…To bleed. My fantasy life merely a squirrel. An upended appliance, I am from a time I do not recognize any of them. My eyeglasses on backwards. Food for the entire family. A blanket of satellite wardlessness, wordless individuals so friendly they can barely contain a name. I know quite what I'm after when it comes to myself, says Zach. There are entire caves filled with people whose way of life does not yet have a name. I am traveling through you, to see you, the time is ripe for a new beginning—a final sense of freedom. Let castigation be my only true sin.

The thought burns a spider into the back of the mind. Cherished image of thoughtlessness all huelike and beggared. My brainchild your abdomen. To be working alongside shotgun shadows, it's all right you're lonely. A million dollars to wipe your ass today, you deserve to be groaning. A backwoods smile. Shattered the limbs, her steel pain. Then black hair meant soothe the flow. Your maturity vixen all right tonight. We keep cats around us because we just can't believe an animal could be so responsive to our warmth! We are animals too though and when we open up our veins, we all look the same. A powerful bloat of honesty. I figured it hurt her more to be a superpower than a dandy. Let Christ into your thoughts, he said. That gold dress must've once belonged to a drag queen.

My stuff is grandiose but also tainted. You can't blame me, having no real religion of my own now can you. A fallen voice and that's what *really* matters.

They put us next to the laundry room. Zach picks up the phone, calls the manager downstairs, hangs up the phone as soon as the gentleman answers. Wash machine does rumba spin cycle madness oh god. Photo of bloodied dog stares outwards at me, those awkward hopes. Lukas is masturbating in front of the mirror. Sometimes Matthew sings Peter a song and there is too much to be reviewed, asshole. I can't let it wait. I need holy penis to float beside my hair. Peter's panicking. The revolution is too much for him. He asked for it on the face, wonder if he was disappointed. There disjointed voices, my merely-go-round of thoughts. Could've used the word number instead of song. Now Matthew will come along.

A cat came into the motel room to help Adam write. The cat emptied its bladder on to the page. Adam continued writing. Pasta for lunch? Sure, why not, there's nothing else. We do what we have to to taste the machine. Acclaim is golden, that golden leisure you hurt. I'm going to wear everything I can before my neck falls off and I'm given a brace. Show up for more information. It won't be long till I see you through.

The cat spoke to him. The stupid cunt knows my name, Adam cried, what am I to do. I don't know who he was asking. In a sense, I've largely given up. Can you blame me? There is a certain stereotype, a fable of yellowed boxes. Then there are holes that do nothing but signify. We won't let them out, let those holes out of the box. They will form a coherence that will work against us. We must fight to see ourselves freely once again.

Says Zach, You're living in a fantasy world if you think this is a moment for promises. I shop at a store where all food requires just eight minutes of heat before consumption. It's the Eight Minute Store. Taylor calls a meeting; future looks bleak. Friend is supposed to be someone you can rely on, to use the bathroom with. Who's that supposed to be.

Says Lukas, I feel like life is a long drawn-out clean-up process; maybe move somewhere else?

This motel is fine for the moment. It offers state-of-the-art amenities in every room, such as air conditioning, a mini bar, cable television, a coffee machine, hair dryers, phones, bathrobes, safe deposit boxes, and free wireless Internet. Pictures of famous dictators on the wall. How could you go wrong?

The delicate art of not-knowing. I love this hour, when it is dark out but all the windows across from me still have their lights on. You can discern the clank of silverware somewhere across the way, even over the loud gurgles of the washing machine next door.

I was never good at finishing things, said Arnold, teary, but he, he could scarcely begin them.

I want all the ugly children of america to take turns fucking me backwards.

CHAPTER 13

The Suiciders

at the ZOO.

The Snot Burglars invade them.

The Suiciders

in the

squirrel forest.

O h look at that tragic drag queen standing over there that makes me so sad but I know I'm crying for other reasons she must be on welfare or something. It would be better if she was cos at least then she could afford to fix her matted-down cunt hairs. She smokes crack for breakfast in the morning cos her dealer accepts food stamps. Then one day she got AIDS and then she died.

The boys were moving along so tragically. They no longer had the Whore with them. The Whore had to go get a sex change operation to see inside her own future. A railway car is worthy. That's where they would hole up, spend the night. In the middle of it Lukas screamed out at Zach's ruthlessness. He wanted to penetrate a veil, but there were no muslims present. Adam had a dream.

You want me to rape the goddamn turtle? Is that what you want?

Stop it, mama, stop it!

I couldn't find the thing he was after. There were too many of us in there at that particular moment in time. A string of clichés run through the amplifier. It happens that there are moments. I am wanted by you and one goddamn highfalutin gun. Arnold's identity as a bitchslap moan. Arnold wasn't there to be defended.

I like it when it's quiet because at those moments I can see the colors. All the world is outside me; we finally made it to the zoo.

I wanted to go directly to the section with the antlers. That's how I'd know the answer to the question posed by the second book of our suicide bible. Before we had a chance to get there, however, the snotnosed burglars invaded us.

It all started with Zach's manic elasticity fallen off trombone-like on the pavement, where it cracked the porcelain wafer. Oh my god, screamed Adam, I knew you were really my mother. Adam was confused. He's not supposed to say things. It's because there are silent forms only the thinnest of us are crude enough to handle.

I told Adam to get away from here. But the snotnosed burglar inside made him take out a red marker and draw a picture of dead princess's abdomen on the side of Lukas's shoulder. Lukas squealed petrified but couldn't move; there was a snotty burglar inside him as well.

Just then, a famous emotional person strolled by. He had all his friends inside his pants. Hey guys wanna come over and dew-ride the catastrophe vein with us? Oh no, my thoughts are transcended, I must now invite someone else to be me for a day.

My thoughts make me feel alienated because they look nothing like fashion.

Matthew or Marc didn't pay too much attention. So did Adam.

I went out back to where they kept the giraffe shit as part of a research project in which giraffe shit would be blasted into outer space as a means of combating the alien life form that used to grow inside us before the government developed a secret method of externalizing it. Zach had instructed me to install a radiation meter inside the giraffe shit that, when deployed into the space zone known as outer, might possibly fortify our suicide satellite into mass catastrophe sphere. I don't know who else he told this to, but I know how few might listen. Thing is, how could I trust that the words came out of that thing I know as Zach or if it were merely a snot emission from the burglar in his brain?

The questions not worth asking are the only ones Marc answers. A savior called Lukas's mother.

The giraffe asked me to go away. Sometimes it's hard to shit inside the silence. You need a radio on playing the world's feedback. I made an address book out of elephant skin and sat on it. The knife is deliberate and now Peter draws an organ.

I know what I smell like, okay? I don't need that entropy to broil you. I don't know if it can be permitted yet. I am having an orgy with myselves tonight.

Adam and Arnold were best friends. They shared the same ideas, the same outlook on life. The same brain, the same name brand identity. They were all but two inside each other on this day. Adam and Arnold had a love affair, they believed in the idea of silence. Arnold and Adam weren't gay, they just had the same name. Adam and Arnold loved each other because they were friends. They knew how to play the game alright. Adam and Arnold wanted their brains to be fit for survival. The world is cruel and I have a nail file. Adam and Arnold were the genesis of all creation. They got invaded right around the same time, their identities very nearly matched. They could've had anyone, anything, but still they stayed the same. A mark of integrity is never dear, it is only held up as a circumcision scar to remind one of solar defeat. Adam and Arnold were in the sky together one evening. Adam and Arnold sold the stars. They didn't believe in defense. They only wanted the country they founded to match the structure of their shared brain. Arnold and Adam had no lovers, they only had themselves to blame. Adam and Arnold were one and the same.

I thought you might like to know which way I was going with all that. The giraffe went inside my left nostril to pick blueberries. Giraffes don't have many coats inside of silence. My butthole is trembling to know you.

Matthew's friends ran away from him. They wanted to go to another zoo. The one they were at simply wasn't good enough. Some zoos have larger feeding areas that the public may fall into. This means inspiration can never truly be organic lesbian. The mercury in a thermometer has so much vision. I want my dog to know he has a father.

That dog had so many friends. Among his friends was the tragic drag queen. The tragic drag queen had never known a zoo. If she had, she wouldn't know what to do. We can't bring her there to the place where the giraffeshit gets gathered, because we all know she'd only run away from it. Truth is usually there as well.

The one thing I really liked about the zoo was the radiance given off by so many of the bulbs there. I think you have to know something in order to be admired by it. A picture of myself as a mental retard. Are there any Leibniz biographers in the audience tonight?

How come Matthew got lost in the dusty paradise. I think Lukas is in Adam's porn star mother's birth canal. He's doing a scientific study. He needs the wind to traipse through it. Ecstatic folk music plays from the window.

The Whore had to go away and fix her matted-down cunt hairs. She believed in the notion of identity.

Jesus has hair too, you guys. You only see the feathers?

I used to be a person I could admire. But that person got invaded. Now what am I supposed to do to get him back. Masculinize the feminine? I think it shouldn't be too hard to become a whale.

The witch doctor told Lukas to paint a picture of a zucchini on an actual zucchini, then cook it and eat it (the picture).

Zach and Matthew decided to go to the zoo's refreshment stand in order to eat a hot dog. This zoo is special, said Matthew, the hot dogs are made out of the animals they keep here. Really, said Zach, munching into his dog like the motherfucker that he was, damnation is nothing but rural apparel. It's okay, you're fragile, said Adam, who had suddenly appeared from beneath the picnic table, where he had been picking up bits of other people's drooled animal pieces. I'll be making a cockring announcement on the zoo intercom in eight hours.

The snot burger invaders chased us around the zoo. We had to run run run so fast, it was like oh my god and shit. Here comes someone else to do. Adam give me your ray gun. He tossed it up the wrong alleyway, Adam and Arnold ran away.

Jesus was hiding in the lion cage. She had an allegory to defend. We all wanted her to win. We were on her side in ways that you couldn't demand. Laser skin surgery is only recommended to individuals of a certain class. The dwarf version of my best friend. He just deleted my boner from the social networking site.

Adam is chased around by an army of angry anteaters. The snot burglars who invaded him made Adam jump inside their cage and wave his dong at them. The anteaters got mad. They felt like they were being challenged by a hierarchical structure that they couldn't properly understand. The answer, as always in these situations, was pure violence. There were no other ideas to shed.

Adam runs around crying. Arnold isn't there to save him anymore. Adam wishes he had a new identity. He wants to have his friends come backstage and rescue him. A cat with a mohawk jumps inside the anteater plantation. The cat distracts them from the chase and Adam is able to jump into the canal. But then he realizes he doesn't know how to swim. Last night I had a dream with alligators. It was so sad because they ate my cat and I wasn't able to save him, I had to run away from them. Adam wants to go back to Florida.

The Suiciders were on vacation. All they had to do was close their eyes to see it. Here comes a minivan to drive away the spiders inside Matthew's brain. Bearded man from the forest comes over to the zoo bench to tell us all a story. When he got midway through, he was interrupted for not having the right clothes on. They tossed him out like yellow molten sherbet in the motel beyondness. There are various things to be told and lightly.

Here comes a sallow rain. All the animals will finally get a bath. There has been a drought for so long, you simply cannot imagine.

It is not in your realm today. Where's Taylor been all this time. There was a rumor floating about that he had gone back to Florida to ask his granma's forgiveness.

Taylor was in the backseat of a stolen vehicle giving Zach a blowjob when the others caught up with them. Matthew had a balloon which popped as soon as he saw them. What the fuck said Adam I thought that once we got to the zoo there would no longer be any need for sexuality in this dream narrative. Taylor tried to talk but his mouth was full of dick. Zach said I'll answer for him. He never did, though.

In the squirrel forest it was nighttime. That's where they decided to spend it. They needed a mode of relaxation that a motel just couldn't bring. To be in nature and attacked by nebulous lightbulb squirrels at any instant. Oh god, what's that scent coming off your foot. I think it's an energy rainbow, Lukas.

Lukas's new friend was Adam. They told each other a secret just the other day. When you want to, we can be friends too. Taylor was sad because he was in a satanic cult. This is the thing that had made him gay in life. Not some other survivor.

To be homophobic is a victory with lightbulb squirrels singing the chorus. Did you just rape that vaseline jar? Shut the fuck up Lukas go find Peter. My friends are all outside me now. It's tough being there at times. Zach in the anal laboratory. Some girls came over and wanted to have a party. We told them we would have to swallow them if they didn't disappear into a clearing. What's more poetic than the face of god getting shattered with a sledgehammer. Only an enormous placenta and the light fingernail tracings of a southern slavophile.

Can you pretend for a minute that you're not of this century, he asked me. I asked him to stop sitting on my handgun. Here is a fire, let us warm our hands by it. Tell me the story of civilization one more time, I am desperate to know what we lost out there.

Lightbulb squirrels are gone now. Bearded man has led them away. But we, we are here to stay. We have so much invested in this moment, it would be a shame to waste it by staying awake.

Adam drifts off into the willows. Zach has a pink endorphin pillow. Taylor lies next to him, scared to be alone. Lukas calls out into the forest through his megaphone. Peter pees into an empty car. Matthew mentions that won't get him very far. Peter says maybe I'll pee on you. Jesus H. says I don't want you to. Jesus I didn't know you could talk. And I didn't know you knew the difference between speech and a squawk.

CHAPTER 14

The House
vs.
the other america.

The White Nothing.

I imagine myself in the circus riding all the animals simultaneously. There's Zach on a zebra, Lukas engulfs a monkey, Adam has an anteater. We can't re-write the adventures we've already had, time won't let us. We blew up on the side of the waterfountain. Taylor wants to take us all down to Sleazy-Livingville. You can't blame her for being a sex change fanatic.

Oh, the rusty snow. We wanted to get away from servility. A chiaroscuro divinity. Show me your camera. There aren't anymore settings on it too real for school. The only words I write down are the ones I'm too exhausted to imagine. Here's Adam, working on his latest masterpiece. You have to get more organized before you fornicate the parrot.

There is nothing to eat here. There is only solitude, which cannot be eaten.

A representative from the midget porn stars' union came over to take our temperature; we were somehow back at the house again, changed men. A legacy we couldn't escape. Something doesn't look right, dickhead, you're bleeding. All of Lukas's friends were on holiday in the other america.

Whales inside your mind.

There are certain forms that can't be called formative. Adam went over to the empty book shelf to get the manuscript. Inside, he'd find the designs for our favorite vacuum cleaner. We were going to build a house and call it a whirl. No one could tell us any differently; we weren't children yet.

Adam reads aloud a description.

Pure being, whatever that is, delicate maneuvers crashing dishes on to sandstone and the ensuing farce. That last one, he of the unknown emotion, wheel so free, be the bird to fly through my brain. Cryptic albatross o to bear it, the times have been wound around your neck like the umbilical cord that was never properly severed, but rather still choking every attempt at loose victory out of you.

Taylor begins to cry softly.

Coming from out of left field once again, ugly transition, just sitting there, feel yourself known. What do you go looking for every day and what is that look so vague, what is buried beneath there, what is hidden that can never be found. Operating purely in the imagined dance of language, seething with that which is not visible, not at home gone to war, the colony is empty for the coldest season…

Taylor says, He does not see you, he's blonde, and there is not another identical.

Who, Lukas? That was Zach.

You will continue seeking, he said, it is a fruitless effort, doom yourself back to the bitter brigade, reigning homesick on the horizon. You are at home though, home is where.

Oh yeah? said the midget porn star. Well I'm capable of poetry, too! Then he ejaculated all over Adam's foot. Adam sat there, indifferent. He had a lot of things on his mind. Things that we can't go into. He was conspiring to overthrow reality. He went into the kitchen to make homefries.

I don't blame you for being old. I would be that way, too, if I thought I could afford it. As soon as they de-regulated our species, said the porn star, we had to fight to keep it up in their field of vision. For the pornographic matrix isn't merely a field for singing sensations, but for us little humans, who tend to scare the industry honchos, as though we were the physicalization of their tiny trembling ambitions, it is a means of movement through a fold.

Taylor wanted to go back to Florida so bad, he could taste it. He just didn't know WHAT he was doing in those boys' house! He knew nothing about midgets or pornography. He came from the south. He was so pure. He had an angel mustache tattooed on his shoulder. Adam came over and drew a face around it. Zach instructed the midget porn star to go wash his penis off in the sink. I'll have to climb the stairs for that.

I don't believe in a coherent system. That is my right as a person whose morals once fell out the window and landed in some girl's hair. As we stood on the porch, thinking of how to get rid of the midget porn star in our living room (did he want a cash settlement?), we felt something. Something as a collective unity. Something I always craved and feared both at once. I knew it was upon us, I knew so hard I could feel my kneecaps quaking in time to the rhythms of my digestion. It was the White Nothing, and it was here to stay.

Nothing comes in a multitude of colors. Pink Nothing is there in our evening fatigue. Green Nothing is what happens when Jesus H. catches a flea in her feathers. Orange Nothing is daytime exploding into brighter day. Black Nothing is much of what we had been in prior to this moment in the narrative. Red Nothing's of the sort that can melt your sunglasses right into your skull. The White Nothing, though, that's something different. Only teenagers who'd shat their souls out in Color TVLand were capable of recognizing the odor and subsequent onslaught of the White Nothing as it began to drift over our luxury slum during that seasonal lack.

Adam came running out of the house with tuna fish sandwiches for everyone, screaming all the while. He likes to go a little bit insane whenever he cooks something. It saves him from spilling his remaining eye into the monotony of the endeavor.

I'm not on fire tonight!

To go home and have sex with someone who is just as tall as you are. It must hurt being you at times. The midget adjusted his height to be just as high as the rest of us. Luckily, he didn't have to compete, as we were all the same. Why is it that every single goddamn one of us in this room has black hair. If I went back to being blonde, would I feel any lighter?

Ferocious buttcrack is plumbing on down. My insipid spider, says Adam. Adam is a demented freak. He forgot where he put his pet spider. Now he's in need of a new narrative.

Scrotal definitionism, the mindblogs fierce. Here is a tong letter to keep your level of hopedefeat from wilting too scissorlike. Here a thousand muffins baked someone's raw interpretation of heaven alright. Never leave the house again, it is freezing inside of reason. The queers have sentience. He will never accept no one's responsibility. Here comes a new line, I am taking you all apart in the evening glare. My raw heartache across this ocean, I'm an adventurer, go somewhere else. This dejection. I can't see you.

The snow is holy, a farce. Why am I sad it snows. The parrot knows an emotion transcription. The White Nothing. Some things can't fit our definition of holy can they. I want a new shirt. The boy has a sad expression in his sour eyeballs. Taken apart from here is a distant snowflake. Know the nature and let it burn you. I am a salted terrorist just learning how to use this gun. I can never be yellow.

Why do the men shout outside my window, it scares me to know them. A certain logic I can never come to satisfy. I only know certain things holy. The power of knowledge lies in thought's defeat. Oh I am merely moaning these days. Most thoughts inside of silence.

Do you want to feel the emotion, Lukas? Get away from my face. Her furry eyebrows trap no foundation (I'm talking about make-up here!). Don't cry. Just die. Come over to my house when you want to fuck the sky.

The midget porn star comes outside to remind us of something. Do you want to eat my UFO? I was only a virgin when I lost both arms. Belt shrieks hallelujah huntingbath holiday. I see a bald fag. Where? How do I remember which lie I told, now that I'm returning? I think it should be like that but really it's not. Those gays, they're always having relationship problems. Fidel Castro anal sore.

Here's a picture of my brain after the last holiday. Why does my breath stink on my birthday? Peter interrupted. It's because of all the molten sadness that presents itself as natural, said Adam, alarmed. Arnold has no personality. That's why he hangs out with us at times. He comes over to our house to bring us fast food. He doesn't want any of Peter's muffins.

The person outside almost looks like he's going somewhere. I am jealous. I want to look that way as well. The tits of a martian. But first I must deal with this midget porn star invader.

Paranormalize your interior.

Generative fuckers, Zach thinks, how old are you today? What is the possibility, what you could be thinking? I am always interested in the question of limits, and why is that? Do you think there is something better to taste, to be tested? Dwarfs on mars, they may think of something too, too always to be tested. Maverick fuckers may be thinkers, but too many germs philoso-phize their own stable beginnings, and I start to think sideways and downwards, rather than up.

The White Nothing is talking?

Adam stares at a pencil. You can tell he really expects something from it, an unexpected burst. I want the pencil to stab Adam in the remaining eye. We must put these violent outbursts in the sewage treatment facility. What a way to program your own drinking water.

Here comes a small taste of file. Ready to wreak foundational havoc on the earth's testosterone. Hi samuel, I whispered to my false memory, send me a message. Let the anal violins rise to the level of crime.

Adam's mother had an opportunity for social advancement. She had Adam instead. Adam never wanted another. And now she's a porn star. So this story has a happy ending after all.

The parrot flew down and landed on Matthew's head. Matthew screamed and the parrot dropped dead. There are no foundations here. The parrot's name was Jesus H. Christ. That parrot had a great identity. You should get one one day yourself.

The midget porn star was jacking off to a picture of himself in the sky.

Adam had an interest in something. For that he was frequently punished. Here comes the sex change.

Adam ran over his mom in a helicopter. Total instability is wrong. The condition of China's menopause.

Adam and Lukas were making out on the couch in the bathroom. Lukas stood up to take a wiz. Evil endorphins were sometimes on his side. Nurse sickness, Adam uttered under his breath. I get a chance to be popular every Friday: wild beasts versus christian morality.

Downstairs, the others had decided to tie Peter down to the upturned grandfather clock with his legs spread wide open and throw dishes at his crotch. Peter accepted this as an exercise in meaning. Girl, do my hairnet. Can we watch the news tonight in mexican? Adam's subtropical sexdate just came over. Tell the deliveryman to get away from me. That's not the delivery man, that's your mother!

It's the type of place you go to when you really want to meet someone headless. Self-explanatoryLand? I don't think so.

The chinese pirate had his pants on backwards. Normal reality can be confusing at times. It is too cold for the insects to expose themselves; the prole version of heaven. It's like my mom always told me—if a mosquito bites you, bite him back.

Well, you're back with us now sweetie, so give us all blowjobs as a welcome back present. The volume, I think, was pre-announced. Her hair full of spiders to give Lukas a rouse out of his dissatisfied lair.

Here now, let me make an announcement all over myself; I'm sorry, was that the toilet? Colors tell me who I am, a visceral green so ill-defined, the maybe nexus what a sweetheart. Sometimes there are illusions—they sure do hurt! At others a pale gray orb, a mutant shadow—manifestmolest. Trophies are a sign of pale certainty, oh let's never set another deadline again—we're in the other america now, after all. Absence is a chronic condition—be certain the welders are looking out for it, their chance to begin again bold—how much certainty, how much fortune? I have enough to films to watch until the day I fall down dead she said—wonder when that will be. True, it is a headache—one can only wonder which direction. Those seminal folds, a dream of wires as I'm falling asleep at night, only to wake up to find I am stuffing something in a very tiny envelope to mail across the ocean (do they need my social security number?).

The midget is mad and wants to go home. No one has paid any attention to him for the last five minutes. Truth can be detrimental to certain sorts of cultural figures you don't want to know anything about. Look at your own urine through a kaleidoscope. I'm selling answers the likes of which you'll never be able to afford.

Call your mother's woodpecker in here, Jesus is coming back from the dead. Dead Jesus chased the porn star out the window. The midget had to revert to his former size in order to get a career improvement seminar lined up.

Oh fuck, satan just barfed all over Lukas's mom's tits. Now Adam can't be a porn star anymore. His father's a midget. Wait, I think you're confused about something. I like how there's a logo at times.

Circumstances are trite when you're a lesbian, said Lukas, moaning. Adam came over and gave him a big fat hug. We knew they'd never come back from rehab.

CHAPTER 15

Not quite yet in the other america,
yet not quite yet not in the other america,

we embark upon a progressive path towards
feeling up higher freedom
as the Whore watches us,

not being aware that we are already aware of her
mutation from whore into faghag,
but these are just labels we keep around us to amuse ourselves
when nothing else is there,
so empty yet sacred is this time we call primal
despite our skepticism regarding all middling
linguistic pursuits
that result in pseudo-narrative utterings
in the mouths of
our so-called characters who are
merely figures
according to one theoretical castration that takes the form
of a most cutting glance,
a glance out the window
that shatters the glass as it makes its way towards the

cow that may or may not be raping a poor
underfed sheep,
whose incessant bah'ing may be derived from either
pain or pleasure,
it is so hard to tell as not one of our teenage
Suicider protagonists
happens to speak the sheep's language, although a myriad
of other animal languages
are being represented in this current phase of our tale,
a tale that can hardly be said to break apart
at this point despite the scarcity of the venture we now feel ourselves vomiting forth, a brand new locale
that very much resembles the old, the one of yore
that very nearly ended all of us, but here I am getting ahead
of myself once again in the hopes that
that special feeling will emerge,
that I will awake unfucked and ready to live once more in this
claustrophobic land with erased borders and
black-haired blank-eyed inhabitants, each of which is
a murderer, either of themselves or of the animal within.

Hi Lukas how are you doing oh that's good do you have some satisfaction today? Pilgrim's progress deep inside me, sleeve got wet when I attempted to covet the noun.

It's a swerve. This american nature, its history. Is that a painting or the truth? Don't social network me! I'm smiling at his ambiguity.

I have so much satisfaction today, it should be sufficient to live. Adam gets into that backpack. I have so much concern, I think it's because I'm in love. To be in love with love, your stomach is mutating.

Finally Taylor's mother caught on fire. We melted her in the oval trapeze. She had been spying on us for far too long. You are unallowed, we said.

Zach gave in to his dehydration. In the sun, a cat. Bitches on fire tonight! Let us go to the club. Let us do the dancing. Everything I know has a potential rhinoceros double. People are latent, it seems. The dryhump thermometer just exploded. You can't be mundaned by that hot dog Lukas.

Lukas wants a new personality. He decides to change his life. Zach is such an enigma it seems. He removes all his clothes from the luggage and tosses them all over the floor. I love my baby buttfuck, give me some candy. The sensuality guise is earthly. Come over here prick freebie your reality enhancement hump my knee.

He's avant without the vocabulary, Peter decides. I remember the person on drugs running around the house with red spots all over his face. Taylor went to go call his aunt. There's something magic about unfeeling. The swiss cheese hostess is coming here alright. I tend to alternate being totally lonely with wanting to grow hair.

People are vibrating next to me. I must be in the soup kitchen. Devour his own thickness before shutting off the spam filter.

Would you like me to solve all your confusion for you, says Arnold. I'm a robot, you know.

Were it not for one chance at singularity, we could end a new beginning. I wrote that one myself. That boy whose name I don't know. I would like to be your muslim if you give me a second chance. If you're not naked in my bed, then I probably can't hear you crying. Typical transsexuals on fire. Thank you for releasing me from your album.

He apparently has no problem having sex with someone he doesn't understand. This is Lukas, the liar and justifier. He just crawled into the chimney where he'd forever remain. Someone wants to view my pic online? Turn that limiter *down!*

Frowny navel is in store. Zach's feeling so tight. He calls up the neighbor to tell her her house is burning down. Of course it's a lie, we couldn't dispossess it in any other way.

Here come on now my heart is an anguish. I am writing on the couch next to Adam. I don't want the gameshow to be aware. Anti-social is the name of this pristine foundation. A photograph of my live wire.

Do you want to fuck me or write on my forehead?

His sexuality was so extreme, you could almost justify it.

Don't be scared of love it's only hunting you down.

You're so indie dangerbox. I wish I wasn't so interesting.

Oh I don't remember what I could have been. Only primordial android—the answer to night's soup. A sudden hierarchy emerges; stab it down. This is not the place for forming answers.

Lukas stares intensely to make everyone around him nervous. He is only nineteen. Dead dwarf awaits him.

Size should never be caught up with ambition. To do so is waste it. My mirth in the countrywide. Ambition is powder—my depths already plummeted. Fuck my salsa brain.

Throwing books at the radiator host, Matthew. I know who your raw sister may be. Lukas is pretending to be bisexual. He had to get a protein enema to try and be normal again. We have a lot to do when we're robbing the vibrator shop. People are instead of friends. Feel my prison. When will you learn to shave your cock in rhythm to this self. Why, then, would people be so confronted?

I think it was they couldn't control the tonal blonde hyping of those ambitions. And this is why failed utopias make me so horny.

Zach went outside to stick his dick in the snow. He wanted to feel good about himself. Nothing that he did was blameless. Only the same angels at every angle. Those black-haired angels that are so resistant. They tear apart in our hands so lovingly. I have a spirit to set free and I think you know something about it. I want to go to a place where someone else can be blonde. Truth has an erection.

As a faghag, the Whore was average. Sometimes Lukas wished her no teeth, further reading. But such were the laws of mechanics that no one could manifest the slightest truth disorder. It was written all over her t-shirt. The more generative ones. I'm hot-wired; Lukas went to the other america.

As he crossed continents, he thought a lot about his faghag's hair. Same generations moving inches apart. To forage holy is a female singer. We were in debt and doubt to the same movie star, respectively. Sharon was the name she gave to her hangover.

You won't last very long on the upside down cross, he told her as he shaved her. Still, there were names. He dreamed of throwing a paper airplane across the room with a note inside, that type of seduction. Instead, he would hunt her down like the primal retard he had devolved into.

Outside, two dogs fightfuck. When dogs do that, they're generally competing for attention. I don't want your animality. This truth invasion. It is time to let the whirl speak. But I thought that's what we've been doing, Taylor cried.

Truth is a generative pronoun. Holy music gives one hope. The boy looked in through the window as though he knew Lukas. But Lukas, he had already become someone else.

I'm so open to experience, I'm like a toilet, Taylor reflected. He had fallen asleep, underage, in a bar. The police took him home to where no mothers lived. That's when the police really started to enjoy its legacy as a collective unit.

Aren't you happy I'm speaking to you this month. The barkeep was a pyromaniac. She kept messing with the candles when she should have been serving customers drinks. They got fed up and left her there, her fingers burning. That's when she decided to go back to school and finish her degree.

Adam finds it relaxing whenever someone sings in a foreign language. This world will never go away. We may wish its demise, but that is only a symptom that we are at peace with ourselves. I can't believe the size of that window. Trash can smells like unwashed foreskin.

The other america tends to have its own pope. For that reason, you are allowed to feel sorry for it at times. A list of all the things I forgot to eat today. Here comes a second-wave bible.

To test out the metaphysics of wrongness. That is all that Peter, the artist, wanted to do. I think my foot's on fire. Luckily I happen to have another.

I called the police on god. It came and arrested her, Jesus H.'s mother. A golden cockring formed by the avalanche. Here is dead poet hard at work.

Christ's salvation is a painted birch. Christ came back, but Christ snorts no cocaine. Christ has its own problems to deal with. Such as: Why am I a bird? It is harder to do drugs than to stop. That is what is missing in religion today.

Stop looking.

Lukas walked so far, he almost became a nation unto himself. Tonight we forget. We have our own gear to spill out onto the snowy pavement. To the left, please.

I'm sorry I jacked off before you stood. Please dis-excuse my allegiance variable.

Sad salmon song coming back again. How come the waitress in the porno isn't bouncing. We thought about transcendence a lot. There were wrinkles in Matthew's nose. The umbrella pretended to have a mustache.

Are there any sexual demons here tonight who'd like to give me a cigarette?

I don't really know what I think, responded Lukas. Do any of you have an opinion?

Who gives a shit? I have a tan.

Adam as a recovering person.

Arnold was once awarded a blue ribbon cos in junior high school he was the leader of the debate team, president of the math club. Came of age at a time of self-obsessive delinquency, the chic of the time, declaratively, anything your mother had thrown in the dumpster the week before, he'd win that contest, too. Arnold was a winner. A contrary thought had never molested his brain cells. He might go to bars every night, and he gives lots of head, too.

Every day smells the same when you're a gay turd. That's Arnold's problem all right: being around the corner with himself at night. I've got tits supreme—it's a Saturday, Lukas yells out from the middle of nowhere. These fucking bandits wouldn't know how to fuck a fucking corpse.

God's tits were hanging out of his nose.

Adam's still stuck in the beginning of the story. He hasn't yet found a way to write out of it, back to the superstore where he can buy himself a transparent brain. Adam and Lukas and Zach were the leaders of this legend; patients in their own home. Every gesture is deliberate: he, Adam, of the schizo emotions. I want a new home, Lukas said.

At other times they wrote letters to people they thought they knew, but had never really communicated with. The frontier opened up, no one wasted any time. Peter became obsessed with oxen. He wanted the fog to defeat them all. But there were far too many of them to move; a rumor of publication had gotten into Adam's skull.

Don't you know the truth behind Adam's japanese mother? He thought it better when I wasn't speaking. The schizocentric matriarch made ape noises whenever she wanted someone to call her up on the telephone. Adam with the black hair getting raped in the hostel? I should have had the chance before I took it. Teen portraitists on the brink of reason.

Paleskin the childish sexuality. Dyed his hair black, well all of them did, a giant inkstain on the forehead. The childrens aren't old enough to live yet. Let them get their towels out, wrap up their lives in spite.

Lukas and Peter and Adam. Matthew and Arnold. Zach and Taylor and Adam. Peter and Matthew and Lukas. Adam and Matthew. Arnold. Lukas and Arnold and Taylor and Adam. Then, of course, Zach. Adam and Zach and Adam. Taylor and Peter. Arnold Adam Zach and Lukas. Lukas Taylor Lukas Taylor. Peter.

The other america came to Peter. It wanted to send him to an outer space whirl. The dinner's schizo. Adam's mom forgot the plates. No one says anything. The room is electrified with the awesome energy of absence. Chapstick stains on an empty wineglass.

The camera moves over now. Moves across the room, I mean. People speak, absence happens. No one blonder than me is allowed to be speaking. Schizo absence becomes a field, a chateau. I am dancing still side-by-side with your brother. I become an inner attachment to Lukas's brother, who was born without a name. There is more mustard than fabric. I no longer like the taste of this wine.

The Whore's absence had meaning. Faghag gangbang number seventy-six, the show trial. Each year we will make a new one, until we no longer have the power to create. The Whore's hair had a graceful bob to it, glacial the palace eyes.

I don't believe you're no longer a fag, she said to Lukas.

True, Lukas had yet to shave most of the blonde hairs off of buttholeland. He was a class act, really and truly. At times he wore a blue sweater in order to feign bisexuality. Every one around me knows what they're talking about, it's so goddamn annoying.

Taylor decided to go hang out at the local gay bar so that he could learn how to be cool. The girl with intelligent hair just came up to him. She wanted to ask him what to be, but couldn't find the words. They bobbed their heads in rhythm to the punk rock song. Then they went off to the bathroom together to experience maximum penetration.

Meanwhile, Peter had lost himself that night inside the elephant house at the zoo. The beauty of that experience, we all want to fuck. Peter was saying friend substitute is a dead end route. The elephants would wake up the next morning covered in insect bites.

Sometimes the key is just how to expedite the waspish process. Do you think I have a disease. The Whore has her tongue in the mouth of another. The old man wishes to recapitulate. Allergy to fucking as re-explained by humid moralist.

The closer it gets to raw is sure. Then children were boring. Could you blame them for wanting to get closer to the prostitute's ether? When I say debased, what I mean is higher feeling.

Lukas wants to come over, he is calling on the phone. Zach scratched the thermometer. Lukas is calling calling. It can get so annoying to hear a phone ring.

An anemic country, a teenage sex date interrupted. People who are too young to fuck are also too old to breathe. You know I become a teenager whenever you fuck me.

The Whore got into a fight with the swiss cheese hostess. They both thought that Matthew was the one. They didn't want to send him into the outer space vibe, and they didn't want to send him into the third version of Switzerland that they had just downloaded, either. There was only one place that Matthew of the margins could go to, and that place was marked on the map in the Suiciders' kitchen with a big fat letter Y. Teenage masturbators go on holiday. There's no identity.

CHAPTER 16

The Suiciders
in the other america.
Adam's porn star mom.
The Whore changes her name
to Tina Turnoff.

Now. When you wish to evoke something, what's the best way of going about it? Some of the youngest members of our listening audience might be asking themselves whether the extent of the erstwhile confusion may be blubbery or merely scientific. There is no answer to transgendered questions. A property is always a bold expression of someone else's non-desire.

Adam went into the other america to go eat some nachos. He knew he didn't really want to be there. And so he went somewhere else. Adam's porn star mom built him a throne in his bedroom to sit in when he was much younger, a child. Her pussy bled all the time, she needed a distraction. She found it in the way men looked at her. Ease yourself off the toilet lightly, I have a new set of values I wanna play with this year. To just become another person is much easier than to assess the value of a piece of land. I am begging you to rape my income level.

There were still patches of unclaimed land left in that nation, whose borders zigzagged around, forming a shaky circle of plateau that went great with her silk dress. The blurred lines all around us, we weren't that eager to see through them. There weren't others to look at, however, at least not others who, in their ugliness, could be considered as attractive as us. We were lacking values, of course, but so was the nitrogen. Adam's mom got naked and went into the ocean.

Taylor threatened to get away from us all. He received a letter in the mail announcing his acceptance into the butthole college. Zach knew we wouldn't be able to kill ourselves without him.

What I like about Lukas is he has such a great spirit, even though you can't always smell it. I want to go inside you to feel up a new rainbow. In the other america, Adam had a name. The spoils of this landscape were blurry. No one knew much about how the game was to be played. All we knew was how to ride it softly.

A multiplicity of oneness is all the glue he needed to get away from her. The Whore. She had her variables in the wrong egg basket, which is how she ended up in the middle of the landscape painting. The landscape painting versus the other america. She wanted to be two people instead of just one. She had her ambitions, they were hardly private. She needed vaseline to accomplish most of them. But they were hers, and what can hardly matter, when in a non-socialistic environment one can own their own ambitions. Follow me calmly, you are a bitch, I am a wafer.

A memory of a motherfucker like a wanton variable. Adam and the Whore were riding horses. The Whore decided to change her name. She didn't know what she wanted it to be, she didn't have one. And so she had to go looking.

Looking for a name in the other america, she had to buy some chewing gum to get through the notion. Her hopes were all chinese. I want to release you from this naming. Adam was only trying to be helpful.

Zach was very communistic. He wanted to liberate the people from their own fears. They would do this by learning to kill themselves. This is what they do under capitalism, only it takes a lot longer.

The elves who used to live in the other america were annihilated by the extreme settlers that had landed there a couple decades prior. So many of them wanted a prostitutionary wave of ambivalence to nullify their transmogrifier. They bore chirpy weapons that fried everyone at first glance. The Whore got down off her horse and a doctor came up and immediately offered her sex change therapy at a significant discount. She had to shoo him away. The sex change therapists are extremely aggressive in the other america. It has to do with the local economy.

Her hair had a vibrator in it. She had to go to the bathroom, find a mirror, anywhere, anything, nowhere.

Zach tried to send Adam a text message. But the service won't work when you cross that border. Syrupy mother armaggedon constant. The children have all flown airplanes. This is quite common in this land. It is the main source of transportation, and only children know how. The sky might resemble a chaos, but it is much better than the horses on the ground. There are no cars, we had to leave them all behind, they are not permitted here. Only horses and airplanes may be used as a means of vehicular transference from one state to the next. Adam understands these things; he has been in the other america many times. Though never alone, always with the others. This time, it is only he and the Whore. That nameless being who just can't seem to vibrate in the right direction, at least not in a timely fashion. Your teenage face is about to fry; motherfuckers on ice.

Adam's mother came over to the other america, he didn't want her there. She hadn't been invited. This was between him and the Whore. While the Whore was picking flowers, they had an argument about it. Adam stomped off and went away. Taylor came down as a replacement. So now, it was just Taylor and Adam's mom and Whore, who was picking flowers in the field.

Adam's mom had no ambition in life, which is why we all loved her. She was the role model for a chosen few. She had her direction, and it was always diagonal-down. She wrapped herself in christmas lights year-round. She had a sense of things like a little yellow plastic bottle. Adam's mother tore into all three of us—me and Lukas and Adam—on a steamy july night back before the weather reversed itself, in accord with the continental re-alignment that was to occur the following fall. By the time Taylor finally joined in, sexual neurosis was not merely key to all endeavor—it somehow lifted us out of the manhole blender that threatened to shake our proverbial milk.

Oh there's Adam feeling so much satisfaction. We can't reach him cos he's crossed the border back into that other whirl. (Whirl is merely world without the d.) I only jack off on your hair when you're sleeping at night. Wide awake is to blow the salacious oligarch on a misfit plateau. Smell you sideways?

She threw up little beetles from her teeth. She wanted to sing but the bugs kept pouring out of her. She didn't know why her suitcase was so heavy. There is so much confusion in a field of flowers. Freedom is something that nature steals from us when we're having a hard time with life. A bullethole-studded lampshade in the midst of the field; the Whore went and sat under it.

Nameless Whore, you are so filled with protocols, I can never give you the tan you properly deserve, the lamp whispered to her. So then why am I sitting here, the sun is only millimeters away. Because now I can protect you from it. The sun being a copy of yourself. The sun projected? No, you don't know me. We are only astronauts. After all, astronauts must get naked too, before they blow up all sacrilege. Once you're on the outer space circuit, as Matthew once knew, you can't get off on xeroxing someone else's face.

Taylor went under the lampshade too. It was dark and he needed light to write Peter a postcard. Peter was out there as well, in the night, only on a slightly different planet. The chief alien there, a loner with a boner named Zach, had certain ambitions that the others must uncover. To do that, we must court the standard lie of dutiful interpretation. Your psyche gets wet, you eat a pear. I want muffins, muffins supreme, Taylor whispered to himself, tears running down his face.

Just then, a dingleberrylike ruckus was heard to unearth itself from Taylor's left earlobe. He cried out in cemented satisfaction before pulling a tripartite web right out of the lobe, har har. What's Adam's pet spider doing here?

If I didn't know you, said the spider, I would totally fill out the online application to become your slut. I would take pictures of myself naked eating strawberry ice cream and e-mail them to you so that you could jack off to them on the way to school each morning. Why the hell did we come to the other america, it's humid here.

Adam's mother needs to heal her isotopes. The climate is good for that.

There was just another deluge of thoughts rushing down on them. The wind is elastic, give me over to the psychos. Back before Zach got institutionalized, we were thinking of coming down here to open up our own institution.

How come I was never consulted on the matter, protested the spider.

Feelings got in the way of every decision. We had to stop making them in order to preserve our group trust. Heritage is not something that can be eaten. Well, it can be, but one can never digest it. And that's the singularity of the problem right there. Too many teeth and too many dialects combined, the phone starts ringing, we're back in the protestant horseshit factory all over again.

Some of us cry when eating salad, some of us die when taking our meds. There are no two truths mudwrestling in the anal confines of Zach's mind. His is the paradox every terrorist must face up to when unveiling the curious statement.

Shivers down the spider's spine.

Taylor fell asleep beneath the lampshade and dreamt about sharks. The sky's suicide wasn't on his mind, but the spider watched it. I can't fix myself up, the television's not working. Below sea level, plates were shifting. They all wanted out of there, no one could find Adam's mother anymore.

The next morning, Adam's porn star mother moaned. That's all she knew how to do. She had made a career of it, this moaning. Whenever anyone asked her how she liked her coffee, she moaned. Whether she wanted milk in her cornflakes, moaned. What type of catastrophe she fathomed herself consecrating, moaned. Acceptance, rejection, didn't matter, always moaning. Some people always have the right answer for everything.

The sinister obliger woke Taylor's ass up in a hurry: it was the lampshade spitting in his closed eye. Why hadn't the spider been there to protect him. The answer's a lot more complicated than you might gather.

Dear reader, shit all over me. You all know that the girl we call the Whore was in reality just a fast food slut like all the rest of us, geared to become famous when a mechanical failure landed on her head. She was in the field, breathing. A cryptic diameter all off to one side. Are you leering at me, or just in me? I'm crawling out to be a fuckworthy sailor.

The Whore smeared lipstick all over her left ear.

Hey Taylor, you wanna hold this lime? I'm just cutting up some breakfast. Wanna snort? I didn't think you were out here still. It's been a long time, that's for sure. Where did Adam's mother go?

The only women who seem to have any value in the other america are the ones who don't wear socks. I am afraid. I can see the sky antlers pointing down at us again. The horizon keeps shifting, soon we'll all be upside down. How can I begin to make sense of this narrative when it keeps jostling me in the landscape. I am lying at your feet, god, trying to hold it all tight up inside. Can't you see those christmas lights shaped like a flower stem approaching from anear? Your silence withers as soon as the sock falls out of the cloud, on to the lunar bend of remorse that haunts our least fried silence. Even the frogs croak diagonally.

Back home, the Suiciders sang a song. A novel that is also a band. A cat wandered in from the street.

Wake up Taylor can't you see that the mother of Adam is coming towards us what are you a fucking idiot or something, god. God sucked her off, and now she wants a bargain? Tell her to go to the bank and raid the other america's deposit on lawn oil. I don't need her anymore. I just need a shuttle back to where I goddamn upended myself before this story even began. You hear what I'm saying? What, does it look like the spider is speaking through me? Well you know what else? A sandfly is all he needs to keep himself fed for the day. So go fetch that too, before the inner zoo implodes.

The Whore wanted feedback on her make-up. There wasn't any on her face, just on her ear. She didn't want people to notice her face. That's why she did that to herself. Now the ear was bright as the cause of most life here. The Whore was a sacrificial burn victim, and most of us wore silent robes. Give me the subtitled version of this conversation.

Adam the angry cocksucker came looking for his mom. But don't you remember? She went away to find more bulbs for the christmas lights she's always wearing. She didn't have to come to the other america to find those. They don't even goddamn know what christmas is here.

Your feet are so sexy mom get them off of me.

Please tear your butt apart in silence. The children aren't watching.

I won't jack off with the spider that close to me, said Taylor to the Whore. There are too many possibilities inherent here, sniffling. Guise logic just won't fit. When I can barely see you, that is how I'll know what I can be. People just yell at me because they like my hair.

Here's the shitty devil come running once again, just like a whore. Shit all over her laptop, wanting to shirk her doubts less the coral find her lying on a bag of gems. There's no snort city, no capital in other america land. Just a defined justification for every law masquerading as an exception.

It must smell a lot to fuck like you.

How will she ever pay for her sex change operation looking like that?

Don't talk out loud, grandma. This spider might not look like much, but his bite is stronger than a fox's indigestion. Why as an experiment. A man's how is a wicker basket, my prime arena. Something about her hair rhymes with honesty.

If you want her opinion, she won't want it back. That fat man just sucked a police officer. Some other people have a source of order in their lives. We never found that. We never went out looking for it. We came to the other america looking for something else. All we found was what was always already there: time outside of time. A cheery vibration to be merry about, lore. It feels sudden, to be this violated.

A bisexual hologram looking after me. Adam knew his mom was out there late at night. Christmas wouldn't come that year. It was feeling poignant outside. The children were already at the zoo. The Whore got lost in the other america. Taylor couldn't find her no more. Adam's mom came back to them already. She did jumping jacks in the sand. Jeder für sich und Gott gegen alle. God is your mother, Adam; the pornographer knows this.

Taylor asked the spider something on the way back to the car. Why does Zach always play country music when he's fucking? Because he wishes the girl might be slaughtered. He's gay, you know.

I often think of sexuality as being in a neckbrace.

The teenager has a sense of style maybe. A name can be a proper noun?

I dream of liberty and I wanna get killed all the time, said the spider.

We're not after anyone else's love affair here, said Adam's mom, who was blinking. A practical verb is my answer. (She was after publicity.) He comes from a small town outside of the other america, the spider was thinking when they came upon the stranger, staring sullenly into the dirt mold before him there. What are you looking for, we asked him. I need to find the source of this wart, came his reply half a century later.

A woman knows violence stronger than a man does. She was all over it. This new LP is fabulous, thought the mother of Adam. She had just fixed her christmas lights as they began to cross the border, fully satisfied by the shortcomings of their mission on that late june night afternoon. We forgot ourselves, all right, but at least we all had fabulous new ringtones. Looking into the graveyard box, the Whore fell inside. Please I'm not ready to be the star of my own funeral quite yet! Adam wanted to rescue her but he was too lazy. He let the spider weave her a prayer shawl.

The Whore thought her name might be Tina all of a sudden.

CHAPTER 17

In the bathroom
of the
Civilitory Orange Spot,
a nightclub.
The Pope appears.

Matthew's watching Arnold piss in crummy restroom shit-stained silver ceiling. But Arnold's not aware of any of this cos he's looking up. To him, Matthew's just washing his hands in the sink next to the urinal. On some nights, a drunk bum stumbles into the restroom and pisses in the sink cos he thinks it's a urinal. The cops usually forgive him as they shove elizabeth taylor swastikas up his anus. Not watching his cock spur out yellow liquid.

The shrieking circuitry of filth overwhelmed by the other-ness of death. This is why we never tried to grow tomatoes.

Still, Matthew watches Arnold piss. They are in the men's room, a seedy nightclub, no one is safe, the door safely marked MEN. As soon as he looks away, another framework will be conjured. Best to do this while whistling. Looking down, most of us can find a best friend. Those of us who can't would do better looking elsewhere, a taste of heaven incarnate remaining.

Arnold wants to ask Matthew something. He can't remember what. One vignette among many. Hot sauce at the end of time.

All those girls out there…muttered Arnold, referring to the ones in the club.

Arnold didn't say anything else. Matthew told him to shut the fuck up. He thought about setting fire to something. He was glad he didn't go to school no more.

Arnold wondered how many versions of himself he'd have to go through before he found the right one. He'd had a plan once. Back before he joined this teen terrorist revival unit. What was he doing peeing here. He wanted to be flashing his big stick before the mass media. This bathroom needs some hydration, he said.

Matthew didn't respond. Not right away. He turned away from Arnold to look at himself in the mirror. Man with a mohawk stared back at him. It wasn't Matthew.

They could hear a man on a microphone. The nightclub action in the other room. Anyone wanna give me a new hairstyle, the man asked, and the crowd booed.

Contentment isn't easy to measure, but it can be done. We speak light to avoid the fag drama. Some of us have friends. Others are merely led. Determine the level of engagement. The old man on the mic sang bluegrass baldness. A ballad, called Bottlerape the Pope in the Ass. The audience sang along, drowning in the blue foam of their collective apathy.

Arnold continued to piss, unabated. He thought he saw a dolphin coming out of his cock. Just another memory.

When Matthew grew old enough to make a decision, he dropped out right on time. He was nearly at that point where, like Adam or Peter, he could've lived safely within the domain of his own thoughts. Instead, he married his mother and tried not to grow a beard.

Mustache man is drowning, outside singer proclaims.

The scene sets itself up to be done with destruction. Certain transparent polar processes. Needle skips on the poor sod's accompaniment. Matthew puts on eyeliner.

A pissfilled monkey enters the men's room, offers to piss on Arnold's leg. Arnold says no but we can share the urinal if you need, I still gots a long ways to go. The monkey pisses in the sink. He doesn't care that the police might come take him away. Matthew silently remarked that the sink and the urinal in this establishment look exactly the same; therefore, how do the fuzz tell them apart when making their routine busts? It could be that Arnold himself wasn't even utilizing the correct facility in emitting his own penile deluge! But then there are others with beards and mustaches who are better equipped. Outside, Adam read a book on science.

We stain so sublime, Arnold thought as he unloaded. No gays are better than us, me and my gang on the edge of the Civilitory Orange Spot.

For that was the name of the club.

Lovers wear their gloves when they wish to admit something curious. The silence is so much sexier when it can be punctuated with a nailgun. Zach was out back going after the chinese immigrants who are trying to turn this country on to sin. Arnold was delayed.

When Taylor and Adam get back from their mission, there will be so much focus. That is what Peter and Arnold were thinking simultaneously, distant though they were. The police came and arrested Arnold for too much pissing. They saw it was useless and left him behind, a purple dot on his record.

Matthew wanted to run outside and thank Lukas for all he had contributed to the movement. But then he knew black-haired Lukas would ask for specifics, and he wouldn't be able to supply any. So he continued watching Arnold pissing. He knew that if they put that toilet on TV, the entire nation would try to piss on their television screens. This would cause a national catastrophe not even the president could solve. Maybe it would be best to learn the movements of the eagle. Lukas's mom was a singer.

Suddenly the Whore appeared. Her vowels were all sugary, the relapse. I'm back from the other america, she announced. No one was listening.

The fashion show in the nightclub was run by anarchists. Most people didn't want to participate. They found one or two goth sluts who were desperate. Their names were Zach and Lukas's girlfriends.

Gender limits you at times, it is true. This is something they had all figured out, shortly before the wreath had fallen on their heads at the annual Suiciders xmastime get-together. Here comes a song we militants can analyze while singing along. Sing means complacency. I value your coupon.

Was that my face or someone else's coming out of the microphone? Happiness flowers blooming right out of Adam's ass as he made it across the border. Tears look sexy on young children. Most of us can be found out by the specious verbs we use. Burp.

Homeland is the explanation the leftist gives. Double-coated to deter all meaning. Someone died to give you this radiology. He wants to shower as soon as he finishes pissing. I forgot to take the wrong pill. We're shouting, we're shouting, my cock is this yellow, it's victory.

Matthew fell in love with colors staring at Arnold's penis. The weather outside was a tender shade of mahogany, its leather wisps beating Adam's book-ridden face. The ashtray annihilated him. Lukas wrote a song about objects. The band would learn to play it the next time we got together.

Someone burst in the men's room, a pair of girls, looking to get high. Guy on stage had threatened to beat their faces in with the microphone, they felt it better to run. Zach ran in after them, where'd they go. Over in that stall, Matthew said, pointing with his stun gun. Thanks, man; oh, and by the way, have you seen Arnold anywhere? He's standing right here in front of us. Really? Then how come I'm not able to see him?

Teen transvestite got mutilated outside the club. It's all because of the fight she got into with Tina Turnoff over the correct usage of the word fierce. She got a beer bottle busted over her skull, and then the Pope came on down to rescue her with advice. Lukas was shocked to see the Pope standing outside his favorite nightclub. But then, all sorts of freaks get married to the animal called night.

The Pope and the Whore began to sing. Microphone man came outside, heard them, offered them a chance to share their song with others on the nightclub stage. The Pope and the Whore accepted, so grateful that they'd finally have a chance at pop stardom. TV cameras were there, waiting, the anchormen masturbating behind the spotlights. Cinnamon Vibration was the name of the keyboard player.

I wanna eat your goddamn face off.

I'm too old to be abominable, said Adam to the Pope.

Wouldn't it be nice if we could have an entire day without emotions, Matthew said. But then we would have to have strict regulations, replied Arnold, as his cock continued to vomit. For instance, eliminating all mention of sensitive issues. And before, we would have to have a referendum to determine what those issues were. Emotions would certainly arise during the referendum process. The pain might cause some of us to secede from the Suiciders movement. That's true, said Matthew, I hadn't thought of that. It's not your job to think, said Arnold. As he said that, Arnold morphed into Peter. Matthew looked up, surprised. Oh Arnold, I didn't even know you were here today.

Back home, Zach was having a crisis in the living room. He was trying to prepare himself well for the night, he didn't want to go over. The others were calling, amazed. His absence had caused so much havoc in their lives already, and he had only been gone a total of five minutes. He remembered when his friends had all turned into hairs, and he was glad that they had human faces and skeletons once again. This way, he could recognize them, even when they weren't breathing. A flow of doubts scattered his chairs. One room of the house had three of them, another had an entire stack. This is how we define the edge: when we are in need of a verbal mantra.

Honey, you don't need men in your life to understand you. That's something the Whore said to the Pope, whom she had mistook for a female. The Pope took off his nascent garb to reveal a fine stack of titties. Those are the tits of a pig, Mallorca Mary, said the Pope to the Whore. The Whore had to correct him. She told him what her true name was, and then she offered him a stick of gum.

The Pope's putrid offenses couldn't stop the war that was raging on in her stomach. She got drunk and chased Taylor around the club with a vibrator in her hand. The vibrator fell into someone's drink and turned it into a milkshake. Taylor ran screaming past the stage and into the men's room, where he saw Arnold and Matthew making out as Arnold continued to piss evangelically. The girlfriends of Lukas and Zach came out of the toilet stall and commenced tap dancing on the greasy tiles. Taylor's screams were unmuted by the twin spectacle.

Down in the throat galaxy, Lukas had given up. Adam's hairs would be too difficult to replicate under these circumstances, particularly because they belonged to an animal. It's a racial way of seeing things. A dead thing that lives on all of us. Not one of us was madder than the other. Sane bibles scattered in the wrong direction. Only one way of destroying yourself seems to proffer much value. Holding up your asshole passivity to the clientele waitress, you assume much better propriety than would you unannounce your spiral into self-doubt witness. Yeah, I fucked you good that night, didn't I.

Underground highness shits are jokey. Taylor almost became a tapdance fanatic in the bathroom that night. I wasn't invited over, I was invited under. I was always announcing. The man on the microphone screams get in here. The partygoers had all abandoned the party. They had to go outside and into the bathroom to catch the fantastic lightning display. Sensuality hotbox lingering. I sneezed so hard, I almost made myself horny.

I heart gladness, screamed Taylor as the girls finished up their show. They fled the bathroom when they noticed Arnold pissing. They weren't so used to being around a definition. Some variables are made out of plastic, squirted Matthew.

Squiggle your way out of freedom before you talk to me, replied Arnold, who was now no longer Peter, but himself once again, another. The saddest moment came when the Pope came in to wash his hands and found the sink to be filled with monkey urine. A goat came in and asked him his name.

You just spilled that all over my ego, you clumsy abortion.

The Suiciders were all friends because they didn't know how to speak to one another. This is what made them friendly and gave them a real understanding. To undertake ambition is also dry. Oh, if only I could dance.

Lukas soon grew sick and tired of being a parody of his parodic other. He wanted to call the police on himself, but he knew he wasn't ready. The smell of wood burning is not an imagination. It's all microphone lore, anyway. I want to thank you for being so silent. My jesus fuck alabaster = on alright.

Now we are bold and unwinding. It is decided. Staring at Arnold in the ceiling mirror. Matthew sees himself up there too, something he cannot see when staring at the mirror straight in front of him. A pure candy godlessness that makes the Pope okay. His secret heresy was to not get born under the wrong oak tree, time and again. Our heresy is depleting. Do you think about atheism before ever getting born. Lukas gives Adam a tulip.

There was a time before bleeding, Zach decided, now the point is to give it all a name. But he couldn't be pushed back to the nightclub, even though he knew his favorite circus act would soon be performing. It was time for a new tiger, a certain amount of tightness. The asshole spectacle winding down, he could hear it all the way from home. A newborn child came over to give him the heartattack answer. Poor Zach, a lion in disguise, he was stuck in a bathrobe and needing no justification.

Sensitivity deluge? thought Arnold via his continual pissing. An ego abortion is floating in the toilet like a giant oil spill. Oversee the oligarchic failure, Matthew instructed him to instruct Peter on how to instruct. The Pope's onstage doing the spoondance as his favorite death metal act milks out a celebratory slowjam. Here's me in North Korea.

Teen anarchists for sale call this number. How many of you slovenly have official faces. Marry me righteous on the way back to petting. We're not here, but we're not really victims either. A giraffe came into the men's room and asked to see a picture of himself. I'm not done eating butter quite yet.

Heavy president has no hair. Nor does she need to disdain what the others were talking about. I am only thinking of changing my mind one more time here. I'm what the fashion designers refer to as a process; show me your love token.

You can be mundane if you want to, said Adam to the Whore, we are all open here. They were still outside the nightclub. The crowd had gone back inside. Only one of us here is young enough, they decided. I wanna market myself to you, said the Whore.

Matthew decided to stop worrying about his sperm count. He was chasing other people's girlfriends cos there was no other way to have a spine. In a couple years time, he'd probably refer to himself as a number, anyway. One much easier than Matthew to recall. The blonde version of triumph. A slave to his own reflexes, beyond resurrection. Certain smiles *only* worthwhile. The brown-shirted reflection. Dedication to my left foot.

Three days later, Arnold had nearly finished his pee. He wanted to dedicate it to his grandma, the statue of liberty. Matthew had collapsed over the sink, singing quietly to himself. The ceiling he could no longer see himself in; it had fogged up from all the living they had done. The time was upon them for a new expansion. The nightclub had foreclosed most of their earthly desires. Hopefully this night will lead us somewhere.

As Arnold shook the last drop off of his garden hose, he sang, *I'm the thing beyond human: motive.*

A squid came out of the ether to let them all know something. Matthew wanted to go home, not to face-off with his desires, but to feed his imaginary pet python with some real rabbits. Some rabbits feed off the desire of hidden objects. Others go to Paris to learn to fly.

Arnold says he's ready to go. He wants to get out of this place before the place destroys him. He doesn't realize that outside the nightclub is another nightclub: his own mind. Matthew will have to explain all this to him on his way out the door.

Glass shattered by a mysterious flying object. Everyone looks up, thinks they know the source. But still, there is another question that continues to linger, a question so forbidden that neither Matthew nor Arnold nor any of the others can truly formulate it without leaving all technological advancement behind them in a hurricane of ashes and ashlike countenance.

CHAPTER 18

The zoo

part two.

A riot.

It was closing time at the zoo and Zach was not ready to get out of there just yet. He was in the squid cage trying to have a dream. The dream just wouldn't come. The animal in yr estrogen? Think twice.

In the squid tank he drank so many liquids, he almost had to become something else. Zach had a crisis as being born leader. There were too many others who wanted to know something about him. I can't believe Zach even knew where he was going for sure when he climbed into that think tank. A squid came and had a baby on his face. Come on and grab onto it sweetheart, the chance that I'm growing sweeter will soon expire.

The zookeeper came in to check on Zach's progress. Sweetheart, sweetheart, you don't have the right volume to your hair right now. The squid is not going to be able to smell your dandruff. Zach became sentimental all of a sudden. He asked the zookeeper to bring him some roasted peanuts from the elephant section. None of the squids knew what a communist was.

Far far away, the others were trapped. They couldn't get into the zoo at night, the walls were unscalable. Oh shit, said Lukas. What are we supposed to do? Certain pleasurable boundaries just had to be transgressed. Being your own hype is a bit like having a pole jammed up inside you. Some of them were tasteless, it is true. Others were named Arnold…

A gay recognition cage variable was malnourished. Zach can't get out of this shelter. He called on all his animal friends to help him. A zebra with a sharp mind. My friends were jello by the time we found them at the lake. Browbeating the pompous shark whose fins were graybent on the side of the moon. Paint smells better when it's fresh out of the can.

Zach wants to be a human g-string and make his own TV. You can do that seven days without even hardly pinching the oven. Sally Salacious has a vowel in his name. Bend the narrative further and you will soon give birth to a character that is simultaneously an adverb.

The squid's nephew tried to penetrate Zach's armpit. He wasn't having a lot of fine attraction. Certain mustard bearers came in the shadow. We rock out all satisfied with the spider lives we have crushed on this tender vestibule that spells out her wallless shellfire. Jesus H. always moans.

Adam broke into the zoo in the middle of the night to try and get eaten. That's when he found out Zach was lodged there. He didn't try to get him out, not very hard. He just wanted to find out which of the animals were teenagers so that he wouldn't have to lock himself up anymore. I hate being locked up, said Adam. That's when Lukas came by and plugged his guitar into the gutter and sang electric guitar song to the warblers. A retard is hungry.

Matthew made an obscene noise with his mind. He wanted all the characters to get out of there. He wasn't at the zoo, oh no, not Matthew. Matthew was in someone else's idea of a good time. An idea that had a lot to do with his fingers.

Please that's not my name, said Peter.

In his notebook, Adam was well on his way to becoming a belgian artist. He had all the figures figured out; they were sticks. A photographic cockring in the fireplace.

He took all his clothes off and put them back on again. There was too much honey in his butthole to start a riot. Still, he had to at least try to visit the vice president. A pig was stuck in his teeth. The zookeeper came in and swatted a fly. Every night Lukas had the same craving for chocolate. He wanted to brush his teeth but he didn't know how. He needed a higher power to guide him. He had a sore throat. Adam was diagramming sentences in his mind. Foreigners collided. The zoo hot dog stand.

Peter and Arnold decided to organize a riot. They wanted to give the workers back the rights they had taken away from them. To do this, they would need to build a bookshelf. In a way, they really wanted chest hair. But there are voices inside the mind that won't let you get into dissension without first renting a rainbow. The language of bureaucracy turns certain dicks to stone; deicidal police state something worth mentioning.

The future of democracy smells nice. Pornographic shitheads. It's rather current, this stupefaction. Genetic download can be obscured by last smile at silence. It's always important to be shaky.

The current riot was too goddamn orderly. Matthew complained bitterly to the priest who was standing nearby. The priest was inoperable. He had a pact with god's last name. He wasn't about to get his shoes scuffed up in that homeless teen riot. He had much better nouns to churn.

Every time I get an erection, I say Peter's name. The Whore was trapped at the entrance to the zoo, moaning to be let in. The zookeeper came and told her that Zach didn't need her anymore. Zach was swimming with the jellyfish, elaborating the paradox. The riot's inner lining hadn't yet reached him, therefore he was fine (outside of knowing). By the time the Whore had reached inside his cage, she was sticking her hand inside the feathers of a prehistoric animal. Back before the ancient transvestite had bought us, we were a real band.

There's nothing like masturbating when you're not even horny. I always thought the devil looked better without a sun tan. I mean certain double penetration angels without the whiskers. We can't all be slaves to dirty horses. Certain of rats, Adam became acquainted with smoke. Something smells good with sauce here. I think I like it, but only to defy what's worth liking.

The manic seal is coming back here again, oh shit. Fiber and glass, kiss a junk shop monkey's ass. That joke of a ceiling still seems rare. Let me hide inside what you're doing tonight, says Lukas to Adam. Adam drew a picture of himself laughing at a globe lamp. This is not my favorite product, he said. My dick on acid.

The zoo nightguard came and yelled at them all for making too much goddamn noise. Some zoo people have no respect for sleeping elephants. Not until they wake up and trample your brains out, said the zookeeper. Zach's vertebrae trembled in the twilight. He hadn't thought to describe anything, and now it was too late. Too late to have an emotion at the zoo. I've woken up to think about things once again, are you on an ether trip or what? Put your love affair in my mouth tonight. I am seething with angoissity.

Tell me why I think so extra large about you. A boy drowned in oatmeal, lost in weeds. The cool pattern brought Adam over. He was thinking all voxy, final lost is real and supreme. I mean the unending. Capital virus. Lookalike sinuses competing for an authenticity divide ribbon. Give me that tainted fabric, a thin glass of wine.

Sometimes the transistor radio playing too loud. The gallery arcade, a fart truffle. Miraculated cascade is for certain. Adam told Peter not to politicize his identity any longer. Peter had a hangnail.

The Whore had a russian constructivist approach to gender, which she liked to exploit whenever anyone opened their mouths. How come they got out of there without going lesbian? You must have been looking for a child. We're the Suiciders.

I tore into her spine real good without jiving a name. Spiral light casts its rays on this table, I want a friend. Lonely R&B singer sang a sad song in the naked aquarium. The news media came over to fart on her morale. Why were you never satisfied? the pop singer decided to ask Adam. Adam punctured a hole in the shark aquarium and the media soon drowned.

I went on about it softly vibrating. Pope had been left in the previous chapter without a brain. In the other america, there are no christians. I am leaning out the window sighing.

A suitcase of tan memories. A second-hand shitter. The ashes of all sentiment, processed through a whore's anus. Suicide satellite crashes into Jupiter's third moon.

Wouldn't be the first time foreskin forefront ejaculatory animal got loose in the park at night. But where is the bird, our savior? Are you tonguing me, or are you insisting on singing? Was this your last chance song, or am I another? I know your breath smells like morning dust. If I must, if I must.

Tell me why I just fucking got excluded, Taylor wants to know. Sick psyche has flowers sprouting from its ego. My gratuity is flavorless. The children of god do a fine job of killing each other every year; I have mistakenly taken the wrong pill. A CIA scientist calls out to me in the middle of the dream, Now you will be able to dream while you are awake forever. Zach calls his parents to tell them the news. Then he remembers: they are dead. No one is there to hide it from him. At least he is able to sing a song. Being ethnic, one is never free. He wants to sing about the silence while not foregoing previous thought. Science is certainly a birdbrain song: I am whispering on the highway.

Come over here darling let me get a piece of that fabric. I know you are wilting whenever you smile at me. I would like to fornicate on your last name juggernaut. The Suiciders went into the wild animal in order to have a party.

Did the liquid vitamin just get all over you, Adam asked Lukas. Adam and Lukas were friends. Their relationship was so well defined, it was amazing. A color TV in someone's sinuses. The wild animal they were inside of was a cross between a rhinoceros and an elephant. Here's what happened there:

Jump into sexuality's raw necklace please I need to tell a lie to my father in order that he loves me don't give up fate has a stale bedroom odor to it then there is my mom with a rope she will kill me (all Adam's fantasizing). Nothing is easy, this lifestyle. Most're raw, not baked long enough to sleaze alongside the birds. I want a lesson on self-containment, I goddamn don't understand what it means anymore. Fate is a loser, so is my shithole, call me up and make an offer, I will feign abidance in order to work up the highlights of spring's causes. Immune to praise, he is fettered by pain—he lives in a bathrobe, and the ceiling is never high enough. Only an asteroid shits higher. Trickled-down ceiling lust, there is a time to fuck and a milklike placidity that seems to operate out of bounds. Fall-down convention is flat; moonlight zero sonata boundless. Demote the is in occupance—dry out civilian territory to aid in the roadside interference. Thoughts're broken savages just waiting for the intermediary—the sense of entitlement offered by most won't go far enough to fathom blockhorses.

Do you really want me to fuck you until your hair falls out? I am licking you on high, so fetid and backwards—the roaming saint at any time of day.

Process means delay—when you let it inside, it always shits out the fucker variable.

Adam likes that chunky feeling. So does Zach. The zookeeper chased them out of the mutant's butthole. Shattering the shadow forecast along the way. Time to move on; there aren't too many rays left in the sun. Behind every identity politics is a desire to be normal. Lukas just wanted to be back at home. Taylor said keep moving. Adam listened to him.

Sometimes communist fuckers think too much. It's elegantly illegal to feel that way, so stop shrieking at me through the silence and elect a new entity to transmit these gruesome moments to the stage. A stop must arrive arbitrarily, and if not, then suffer the silence (so relaxing!). Wicked baskets contain no lust. There is only the hint of a tongue, a stomach so far away.

The moment a liquid seeps from the right nostril, we are carrying it along ourselves—grapes deserted at grave time. Happiness salivating itself righteous, the threat never to be sour—I am through thinking through the thorough throat. Lattice-like endeavor another year's striving for lightness translated once again into supposition, misery, forced thought...Rails of twitter turned her bitter. Old friends a friendly fucker, molten pervert twisted by rain and no new trees to fuck (addicted to outside). I want invite-only splatter to land right square in the middle of my forehead, maybe a nun? Misarrangements force by belated husband to form a tree with his knees. The sky is so calm tonight and that's because it is now infected.

The poison shadow: inauguration day in the other america. A feeling that bleeds us so deep, the imagination is woe, sticks into us when we have no other place to go. I can't believe I read through your thoughts like that the other night, a deck of cards. Genius shadows folded up, the inside is the nihilism of decay. I am a foundation? Where is the departure point? Spirit of invention so formidable, I could hardly weigh you down, it stinks inside, no memory I could hardly share you. A very vague sort of love poem writes Adam to Zach, one I am sure the Pope would never approve of (if he weren't still stuck doing karaoke). Mindless examples of some other piety, scattered dots line the alleyway, glad about plenty, all those space aliens I was meant to know.

The dreary throes of space, my friends are a record player, their voices scratched inside me. We can never be alone, we are spending our holidays inside of thought—when you thought to be rotted, then it was all okay.

The knife inside of vagary. Stab out every sensation, no pain of the emotions to lead to self-definition, I am bleeding. I woke up and joined the law, blatherance defines who I am was & will be, you can't help it you fat whore of a former person, the knife scrapes out what's inside you.

I want to go to the zoo. I want to go to the zoo although I am already there.

The cat falls apart whenever the Whore looks at her. What is a cat doing living at a zoo. Seems she smells trouble wherever I don't go. It's a good thing, the smoke pelted out of her eyes. Makes me feel normal for a moment (I know it's all lies). The zoo burning to the ground around us. All the sea creatures leaking out of their aquariums. When feeling happens, the idea is to become a machine. Steal the horses, the night away. Old boring hippies with no past, no history to fall back upon, let the water drown you, let the selflessness of dawn make its approach.

A self is created by society a barfbag of thoughts and emotions, the music that makes us laugh and wonder whether that consciousness is a shared joke or not, am I alone in all this or is this self part of someone else's, a negation? Yesterday Adam jerked off it was August, a phone call on the screen in front of him. People like to pretend they are different, haha, I know what truth is, a huge boner in the cocksuck eyeball. Literature is confusing—so stop it, please, bring to the forefront some higher usage. Promulgation of underlined vowel stream? Earthtone mother upon us headset, never rely on structure. These days to be so disemboweled. Sugar is fire drowning in the water. To what it applies my trophy is discovery, the wooden sandals beneath the fire—I heart you standing.

A description of fire: The strife component blatant when you're stretching toward the moon. Remember to be yourself: an old commandment for hippies. There's nothing new. Only the occasional artificial glare of realization. A sticky component. Strange smiles bring upon us lightning rod thoughts all in rain. The dry symptoms that spell private. Or too many drugs. More nastiness the movement outside that gives out too many brains the day is long and dandy-like. Symptoms on the shoulder how they run away from us at times it hurts so bad to be a shadow. Etchy the primordial zookeeper realizes her face falls off in winter; what to do. Sanitized thoughts get so clingy on the wrappers: face shrinkage makes me think lovingly of a host I once had he was nearly a part of all this life. Vomit mutant orthodox creatures do not let a sense of the real attack you. All this orderless rhetoric to serve a higher purpose. Do I smell ostracization? I think the satellite rumor you dispatched out might have had some unusual repercussions. Namely, there are no more poets among us. There is a holocaust of apathy that leaves us feeling grateful. There are no more churches allowed to interfere with our infernal paradox. Nature goes to the bath-room all over the floor. Systematic warriors brown by the chance that near-atrophy granted before shuffling off—the zero wind. Why don't I make an announcement to the world I know not what you are all about, I swallowed the void and it tastes all testicle. Chimney above farts out dull walrus, the sky neutralizes itself with electrons. Look away from the illuminative display of night. Here is a fortress, does it resonate right now. You think a new name is gonna make you squirt?

There are no eels here.

CHAPTER 19

At home with
the Whore (the House).
How the Whore
ended up in Adam's
empty eyesocket.

Matthew takes a pair of scissors, cuts all the dark ugly motherfuckers out of his life, convenience rains down upon us. Sharks eat raw flesh. The teeth in between his legs. No one cares.

I'm one of the victims of Matthew's multitudinous assault. Peter got caught up down at the faggot junction. Kitchen smells. I took a pill to restore all my previous vitality, abstraction's absence. Wind of the shadow just got eaten. I didn't really think I'd have the lesbionic name to be staying here. After all, I'm fairly certain that *gangbang* is a psychological condition.

Thought's automaticism breeds other intention. Go down to the basement, see what you find there. Taste the simplicity of my anglo-american fuckrod. We weren't moving. A delay in nocturnal. Fireworks abounding.

Where did Zach go? He went outside to scream at the sky. My juice has the potential to kill all nouns and fuck the sky with nitrogen. Adam's in the house writing on the walls. Stasis can be its own sound. Lukas definitely doesn't want to catch fire.

I like what you were almost about back there, the Whore tells Adam. Thank you, Whore, for being such a love affair this evening. Can I buy you a new comb? The elasticity of rainbows is truly something. We were never in the House, were we. We always imagined ourselves inside. The cunning circuitry of lasers.

Matthew has the scissors in his hand, running around the living room screaming. They have replaced the television set with a drawing of a television set by Peter. Adam draws a mustache on the TV. He expects his own face to fall apart now. Those plastic angels he calls friends. Beery eyes all wrapped up in the silence.

The Whore wanted a penis all to herself, and so she sprouted one randomly one day. She was so surprised to find her inner life outer in such a thick tree branch protrusion, she climbed up on to the rooftop and went all virulent. Finally I can do what I've always dreamed of and jack off all over the world, thought the Whore just as she reached the pinnacle, at which point she fell off and landed in Adam's remaining eyeball. Unfortunately, now Adam will have to walk around for the rest of the narrative with the penis whore in his eye. There are other definitions of freedom, I suppose. Some teenagers smell.

Lukas is in the kitchen talking to the biscuits he just made. He puts his face up close and commands them, goddamnit. That's what men oughta do when they're still proving themselves in the morning light. A police state is blooming in the chocolate eye. Growl at those biscuits, Lukas, tell them who the master was. The color yellow makes him scream! Short-winded hysteria as Adam comes into the kitchen getting used to his new means of seeing: namely, he can't see anything, but the Whore in his eye tells him where to go. She has agreed to lease his eyesocket for the duration of his existence. Knowing he'll soon be a suicide, she has her freedom to look forward to. No, that is a lie. For she never liked her freedom much to begin with. This perhaps explains why she took up the only honest profession that exists on this planet, only to find herself kicking cans down an alleyway alongside this teen suicide gang and their assorted detritus. (Movement is always inner; outer is a delusion.)

See the rabid python chasing Matthew down the gutter. Sometimes it helps to have a day off in order to think about all your regrets. I keep thinking it is not too late, I am already wet, this pirate legacy. Dusty dreams on spiders away from here. Look at Adam, Taylor says: spider in his nose and whore in his eye. At least one of us has made some progress since this narrative got destroyed.

Someone planted a bomb in my teenage righteousness, a spark went off in the alleyway. I'm feeling netherlandish today; do you see my eyes anywhere? Quit—what—who is—is it Lukas talking? What could be beneficial is a mistaken quotation. An insertion up to the margins. A buttcake denoted as prime. Feel superficial neanderthal calling. Adam's pet spider has an erection.

Museum fuckers are always astounded. There won't be any news. It often hurts to be reminded how sad we once were, before we came together and formed a unit. Matthew is reading a book on how to train your hippopotamus to sit down. Jesus, he cried. I'm on the other ceiling.

Lukas continued to scream at the muffins, his face just inches away from where the cool yeast gave off its scent molecules. I'm on my way towards seeing, Adam proclaimed. A saint came and reminded him to pray. Spider came out of his nose and crawled up into the vacant eyesocket in order to think about something else.

No sleep until visualization occurs!

Please put my active desire back into your suitcase.

Is that a cumrag or my sweater?

All the motions we go through in the course of a single day, before the sun comes out and slays us. No two motions can be delineated here—vestibules are samey, and the danger lurks behind my turtle shell.

America keeps doubling itself in order to avoid saying something. I can't empathize, locked in my favorite flavor. Away away, the dog. No two teeth have smiling trophies. Gravedancing nazis are on the phone. You see the cheese being produced by Matthew's infected hangnail? Then perhaps your eyes aren't open wide enough for them to fall out.

Matthew's best friend is benevolence. Here, have a tomato.

We will continue being restless until the night. To be thankless is vague, to marry a curtain. Women wanking are dry. The titless surprise is that the Whore knows vision better than the parrot they call Christ. Glassed inside the monkey cage, she offers no more forgiveness. The tits of life and death are not always there to answer.

I still can't believe the words are leaking out of her mouth like that.

The violence has already split her apart.

To de-activate the feminine, we need a motivatory verb settlement. Endorphins flare whenever Zach wanders into the room; we are starting to believe all those myths about violence. Still, there are others to be settled against. Like what? True feeling? We only float when the wakefulness commands us to. Legitimate ego is there to be forthwith in 'standing. Presidential kindness release your own stance. My fucking gumption is buttfucked away from the hammer-prone loveriders among us: this was the Whore's guarantee.

Morbid triumphalism? Or just merely a carrot?

How many baths are too much for one day? Lukas was asking Taylor upstairs in the bathtub. Taylor didn't have a response for this. Just then, Zach came in. Hey homos, anyone wanna watch me eat this here peach?

To be truly against your time, you first have to own it. This is what the anarchist buttfucker teaches us about monarchy. The wooden table dances into the bathroom, breaks up all the tiles on the floor as it transmits its music via motion.

You need something nice and long with a diamond-studded cockring to hold onto while you're falling asleep at night. Lukas slaps Taylor's face.

Moany sanctification, too much humming.

Trembly anal spectacular is all ready. The Whore runs upstairs because she can't stand the sound of Lukas screaming. The biscuits are starting to age. They need a new identity, or just to catch on fire.

Darkness arrives to declaim its visceral message. All cities it touches fall to the wayside, throw artificial light to the sky. Some sacred calling at the shuttle, a loose boy falls out, hurting his brain. Some know no melancholy, others have only their fears to move them through the tunnel.

I got out on the left side, kept thinking about my friends, how lost most of them are. If I could feel all the sadness of the spectacle, I think I'd be lost too, not wanting to go on and on.

Tonight is sheltered by event, action: it itches. That seething pile of alrightness. Hurt reveals. It unveils itself, that glue of foregoing. Here is a spider crawling past the feet of its master. Make a note and post it on the door.

(Picture of Lukas with a snake wrapped around his neck.)

Fartful animosity can't always equal glory. People are vague when you don't know them.

I am not an answer, he says.

I'm seeing that cloud float by, it's so sexy. Can someone else finish this thought for me? Taylor cries from the realm of the bathtub. Dead before I've even begun. Cowboy couple dancing tremulous on the TV screen. Let them go away from here, then it will be safe to speak. The day and if we own it. This coffee kind of tastes like a dick, replies the Whore.

It was the next morning. No it wasn't. Sometimes one finds an excuse to stand up.

Vitamin tastes so nice first thing in the morning. A needling supply? Angst is like anal, so am I. Kitchen announcement bleeds on high-rise carpeting. Here comes betty vestial membranes, a text message you can really identify with on a purely non-emotional level.

Zach thought he was going to apply for suicide grants all day, he did something else instead.

Outside, the sky consists of shields. You really can't blame it for not wanting to get close to us—razor synthesis, the matted-down machinery spills rage alongside the razors. Doubt is never free.

The assertion is what always goes behind Lukas and that's why he is able to understand languages that aren't his own. Spiders crawl across his face most of the time, it is that era. Manic gesticulations make Lukas the drummer that Adam is not, his parent afraid that he runs away from what he already has. The meat advertisements never drew Zach in. Only primordial—those are the drives that lead to extinction (natural). What I am, the masturbator, coast in the other america, Taylor and Adam try best to avoid the mother syndrome.

Plastic pretending a foreign master is there. Then Adam is in the front yard raking the leaves, as though to displace Lukas's screaming (sound via action). Being satisfaction, imitation of, a wicked course. Fatigue what generously allows us to dilate (hey, foreign friend, other americanness can forever its skin to be painted). Democratic conceptions are solution. The hypnosis. Being satisfied. Adam is on the brain windmill comparing colors. That non-christmas green leaking out of fourth finger.

Primordial bondlessness, forge a trophy. Trophy being symbol of mutual defeat, what we're looking toward: ideation. The Whore runs across the yard with Adam's teenagehood in the palms of her hands, winning. She imagines that to take away is to breed forwards. Prime announcement (to be winning). She runs into the forest, where Matthew's on the webcam. Matthew's winning wank: a woggle! Whore turns the forest lamp on, after school special melts on her hairful mound. She has the specious wish; to feel supreme. Lower truly than all the others. He agrees to be unending, he is always the parallel one there, the sword of his soul in his hands!

Time to be erased? The characters chafe at their meaning. Agent called in requesting Suiciders for a gig tonight, start a house fire. Get your dumb kid off my premium cocker. Oh yeah, sediment can be instructional. Adam's so unearthly at this moment.

I want to get used to you so bad, Zach tells Taylor: they are now in the bathtub together, dreaming through the drain. It all gets to be too late—the hour, the collective brainspan. For how can we murder ourselves through this collectivity without inhering a higher meaning-form, oh godville! Hysteria was the thing I specialized in before you invaded our nature. This porcelain soupbowl we find ourselves feeling each other off in is a lot like my horse, actually; pass me those matches. I mean to feel ourselves being free goddamnit. Don't tell me what I'm going after. He got this one particular idea and now he's feeding off it. But this was supposed to be about Matthew. What—the whole goddamn thing? Let him have his gospel, I just bought a new hair straightener. Holistic horsemeat was the only thing on the menu that summer. I heard you were bland? No, but it's what the others are always telling me to be. Lukas is still screaming at the biscuits.

CHAPTER 20

Longitude's necklace.

Upon waking, Zach decided to pay someone else to think his thoughts for him that day. There were so many things he wanted to do. It was never easier to pray than in those unhampered bushful yearns.

Lukas just had a realization. He wants to tongue his little sister's humpy entropy. She's too little to know what forest is. I've already been led down the wrong hallway once or twice. Now I'm giving up to share the silence with someone else's barker. Call security, quick, cries Taylor.

Zach went on to elucidate all the forms of thought to Arnold. There is word there is image there is gesture. We give priority to the third, because it's the only non-static gestation. The way you flex it is often an alarm. Sometimes I write so hard I have to go vomit in the bathtub during. (I hope Taylor's not still in there!)

Q: Why am I so cold?

A: I can't afford a pair of cool-me-down wheels.

Once the Whore abandoned him, Adam had to televisualize someone else's eyeball.

On top of old smoky, all covered with smog, I bought my baby some radiation, yeah she really knew what to do with the dog.

Before his mother came over for lunch, Lukas jacked off in the tacos. Arnold was trying to quit smoking. There were friends all over to help him. Friends not in the cerebral sense, but real entities there to vasten the underwater nuclear enterprise. There is no politics that addresses human desire, which is the place where the animal reigns through havoc.

Adam went into the bathroom and shat out a mentally retarded baby. Blind, he'd never be able to teach it anything in this life. And so he had no choice but to flush it: a lesson in abjection.

The most deplorable sentiments are the ones we genuinely feel. I'm not after anybody. Who can blame me? Adduce the color out of that last statement. Adduce is not a trembly adverb.

My mutant satisfactualizes left, proclaimed Peter, coming out of hiding for a riding. The sore horse had another debate to enter into. There were children on the way. There was a strange silence that rhymed with pathology. The lentils screeched in the kitchen.

Stop causing the fire to come after us! Screech owl is merely a fix. White whale a product also. Smells so lardy to be me.

Hysterical voidance chasing after a leper farm. Your face can't be Cuba also. I am waiting. I won't be chased. I am not added. I am not after a fire. I am the burden of the fire's logic. That sort of tropical everydayness is not my thing, really.

De-invention—the prismatics of obliteration. Is this fit to scale? A mountainous melancholy. Fit painless anal tutorial right up her sheath, the black cat represents whaling time when you get right into it (loneliness). Cold institutionality makes the German want to jerk off. Those from the south find it oppressive—they know what a sweaty dictator smells like up close and personal. I'm thinking there might be another chance to get controlled. You see the fine ashwork the natives have made with their changes.

Maybe the Whore savors the scent of the biscuits brewing. Matthew went to a place called Amsterdam, must ask how his interview went. I am a log, so happy and naked in my spite. Harried through the windlessness, okay to hate me now. It won't be long before the window becomes sacred. You won't let it get to that level papa will you? Legalize gay abortion.

Boy with the lips doesn't want to call me, Whore complains. Adam's eyeball itches. That's what makes me love him more. I talked to him for five seconds, now I'm pure and ghosted. Feverish blades run right through my arm. There is an animal that annihilates most of my fears.

It becomes an angle, a vague. Suddenly the boys found themselves back in the forest again, confronting the burnt black totems sticking out of the ground, magnificently huge, a civilization that pre-dates our crustified language. Let him out of the sorrow camp, he is only a child.

The child, nameless, was forced by the Suicider clan to serve as an offering to the great mystery of the burnt trees. The parents told the child not to be shy, that he wouldn't be molested, merely sacrificed. And the child said okay. He wanted it too, he just couldn't say it. My favorite critique to be one step ahead of the logos. Always the sacred, yeah, my mother's doctrine. I'm always a bisexual chemist on Tuesdays. I'm playing so hard it's like my eagle. Wanna go outside and play?

Dance like a nigger outside of time. All this history has a crude effect on my intestines. Cancer is something I could grow fond of. It's a light blue sweater, holding on. Get on top of me, it's sad, right?

The artificial light warriors are always the ones who want to shatter my face. I can't let them into my eyes, annihilation is certain. The weather is something else. The way the burnt totems radiate their salvation out loud. A new intuitive sense is necessitated, the yearning buried deep within every process. Everything that can be called process. Or processual. Steamy navel. Thoughts viscous and lunar also.

I went down to the western world, someone said my name. Fuck is an avoidance, always. A totalizing statement is oft made. We weren't inside the silence holding out for us yet. Were we to doubt, we would unbridle our names. Here comes Lukas holding a goose liver. He will feed it to the child that we offer to the offering.

Christianity is for saviors, said Taylor, who had diarrhea. He must've been remembering something about his mother.

A song was suddenly broadcast through the forest. Sink the frontier into the midstream, twin infinitives imbued the forest with their gruntful intonations.

The totems replied with purple smoke.

Adam writes all his lyrics now in noninstitutional puddles of sperm. He writes for a dyslexic audience that lends itself well to the interpretive enterprise. What cannot be simplified can luckily always be misconstrued. Bedroom closet of a teenager being the perfect instance to waive a revolution. Ambition likely to stand in the way of petrification. It doesn't matter, you're too far outside the game of chance to fit survival.

Mother mayhem, the tooth that breeds. At my lover's house, cried Peter, shaving. His is an indigenous waxjob in need of a baker. The mirror dilates every time I writhe on it. My perfect object went away.

Smoke continued to pour out from the forest floor, refusing itself all the while through its means of infiltration. The sacrificed child coughed, trying to sound alarmed. In actuality, he couldn't wait to meet the beast that would consume him. We are not living in an era of typical saints anymore. We have to improvise, I am afraid of what submission tells me. And especially what it could smell like.

Being corrosive is such my zero, Lukas asserts loudly, to no one. A pause for rest at the end of an eventful day. Night begins in thirty-nine minutes. Will I get there in time. Now there are no others to rely on. (What a dream!) Are my teeth clean? Lipstick on the ape's eye.

Satan chases Taylor through the forest. He doesn't know what to do, it is such a dramatical moment. He wants to go fishing, but first he must sacrifice the child. This is someone else's notion of inherited defenses. My bottle was scientific before the vulture. One day our animals will eat us.

The child ran in a circle around the totem circle. His life was repetitious, like a word that you want to avoid and so you use it over and over again in the same paragraph. Adam holds Lukas's hand. It's not because they're gay or nothing, it's just that they suddenly find themselves in a different culture.

(Armpit.)

You had those in the other america, Adam reflected: yearning for release. A stomach-fried alcohol. Love comes in different colors; the vices are all the same.

Here come my doubts, all seething and listful, Zach shouted into the forest's hair. Pastels are for winter; winter is for pastel. What my stomach will go through once this is all over, once the child has been sacrificed through the forest's windfall and we have already digested his bones. This proves we're allergic to primordial soup.

Lightbulb bare is my everyday awareness, the lads reflected as a collectivity. What you can do by cleaning up the house. Let's not go back to it ever again. We have to, this is a forest, he said, pointing at the fur-coated trees.

I don't want to queef in L.A., shouted the Whore.

Adam doesn't know before he sits down to re-write it what will come of it. He doesn't need this knowledge; Zach does. An act of instinct. Oh my.

You're relying too much on the things in that goddamn notebook Matthew tells Adam. Fuck you you're not allowed to talk to me like a savior that's Zach's job. I don't want to get ugly on the matter, but this can be all de-interpreted in the order of emittance. Sharpstrained feather feeders are festive in the forest. Floor me, why don't you, the totemic aura is being emitted in the wrong disaster area. The child won't stop circling the circle, soon he will accidentally run a square. We will then be forced to gag on another thought disorder function. Chances are opiates could help reduce that factor, Taylor duly noted.

Dramatic sinking ship flashes its way across my mind. Oh my god, the disaster will be tomorrow. Let's kill ourselves before that is allowed to happen. You're a shitty cult leader, Zach. I think you want us to know something. That sucks.

Shut up, fuckface, before I dingle you back into the reality I dug you out of. Homos don't always have to be vultures. A language is ultimately a thing that cannot be spoken. Sometimes I believe in waves and I want to become a star. Christ is such a ridiculous jew to emulate, I mean really. Don't exterminate my contamination. Fighting the complete picture man, forest gets shattered. The preacher affirmed that he wouldn't fuck anymore children until the second coming of christ.

Ashes would be left where the totems once stood. They simply burned from within. They had been programmed to do so by their ancient makers. You know, creation is sort of like a virus. You have to believe in it in order for it to infect you. Two notes drown out understanding. The way they are intoned from within the forest's floor, they do not harmonize. It is more like a competition, skull-fucked drifter screaming sunday please. Lukas got a premonition to dig, and then he unearthed a shapeless statue made of bronze. Hey guys, we can sell this to help fund our suicide. But the others didn't wish to enter the art realm. Nuclear fart inferno felt better. What's that chinese mexican doing going through my purse, the Whore shouted in her worst white trash accent. Everything in the forest that wasn't human applauded her efforts.

Bitch I know you just stole that silence right out from under my aegis, get out of my goatskin ego before I scan that nametag right off your heart.

Emit me carefully please. I have a hunch that you're not really a crossbow. All across the squirrel, the teenagers traversed new territory. The rot that comes from within always has to be re-directed outer. Otherwise a microwave. Belief a parable too defiant to inhibit the weather machine. I'm not much interested in black penetration by the forest machine. Inner sanctuary defied by dreamlessness. A state without vision; that's where we always dreamed of living.

It's sad that we don't have our house no more, said Lukas, but to tell you the truth, I never liked it much anyway.

Then why did you never leave it?

I never had a chance to breathe outside it!

We were only there in an egoistic sense, thinking about it. Slutty nutjob all in pearls. We don't really want to be stuck in this loveless marriage!

What we were leaning towards, we were starting to come to realize, was something that had to be destroyed faster than we had originally fathomed. Re-inventing the other america, let silence explode into a million heartaches.

Lukas awakens all alone in the forest. He can't find his mother in the pine needles. She was the only thing he was heading towards in those years. Zach came down to find him. He was aimless in his searching, the long while.

Zach got out the soapbox and decided to mutilate the others through his words. The silence begs for another form of silence. The White Nothing leaning in to sabotage his leadership.

Once the child was done being sacrificed, we decided to disown it. Its mother was in the forest searching. We didn't want to lead her in the right direction. We knocked down all of the signs, decided to forge on—some demon's inner lair. That's the direction of the smoke, we all knew. Not the smoke of the White Nothing, the smoke of the self-combusting totems. That feathered logic that annihilates most soaps.

Her heart is boundless, bleeding. She is the porn star mother of us all, the Whore, and she doesn't even acknowledge her own presence once the forest threatens to overtake her human-style longing. She dresses in fur and feathers, leaves and twigs to make herself invisible. You can blend in with nature, which is nothing less than an extended series of disasters, all competing to annihilate us. We won't let it. We will become like nature, and thus win this war, the war against the silence that bleeds in our mouths from afar. High up, the eagles squat over us on the tree branch. Those trees are higher than the sky's own children. We can't own the sky, but we can at least see which parts of the ground have evaded us the longest. Then we will know how to answer these questions. We will learn what it means to ask them. We will go inside the knife blades. We will speak the language of the worm.

CHAPTER 21

In which the House,
the other america,
and TVLand
all merge into one liminal zone
through which
the Suiciders
may tapdance.

Back at the house, which had suddenly sprung back into existence sometime after the last chapter's destruction, Lukas and Adam and Zach and Peter and Matthew and Arnold and Taylor sat and watched a porno in which their doppelgängers cut holes in the sides of squirming shrieking animals and proceeded to fuck their guts out. It was a doppelgängerbänger! A midget rode a horse into a field and shot all the porn stars down, mistaking them for the real-life Lukas and Adam and Zach and Peter and Matthew and Arnold and Taylor. No one had any answer. It was a sad scene.

Suddenly they all realized simultaneously that seven others were watching them watching the porn. These seven others were located in the other america, and the camera behind them broadcast directly into that realm. And these others were being watched by yet another, singular, in a place far off that no one had any access to.

The way that we've been made, Zach broke the silence, is that we all get to remain teenagers forever. Isn't that just miraculous? Hallelujah, I want a ferret, Adam responded. A liquid toad had just come out of him. The tree outside had begun to grow a huge ear. He went outside and cut it off, put it in a socket where one of his eyes had once dwelled. Separate myself from this existence once or twice a year. You're forever hurting me.

Adam's so juvenile. That's what Peter thinks about Matthew, too. If they were truly friends, they would've all fucked each other by now.

Will you guys stop fighting screamed the Whore I'm pregnant. Everyone stopped to look at the father. A lobster came out of her twat that year, it was Saturn. No one was authenticated really. The teenagers became children, running around the house chasing each other with frying pans. The mother of mayhem rose over them in a cloud, spitting forth all her poisoned dilemmas. No one wants to kiss a prison.

Hey Adam where'd your goddamn parrot go?

Jesus the parrot had been transformed into geriatric Jesus. Everyone had an argument. It's because they'd never fucked. They'd never fucked the parrot, they'd never fucked themselves. They'd never fucked each other, they'd never fucked the elves. I thought this goddamn house had been destroyed, what are we doing still dwelling in it. Peter doesn't want to go to the other america.

Peter has a lot of things to do this year, this life, this enterprise. It's not all about yelling. There are some disenfranchisements that smell nice, also. Once I was in a café thinking about something when a bell rang out. A chorus of anteaters emerged from the kitchen and were forced to tapdance while an evil witch whipped them with an electrical cord.

Adam was in the kitchen, twisting some pins into a mound of meat (not his own).

The Whore was never delightful. She hadn't been able to feed herself with a spoon until the age of fourteen. Once that happened, she was allowed to stay that age forever by the priests overseeing her development into whoredom. When Taylor came into the kitchen, Adam screamed out it's not ready yet you doofus! Oh shit, there were elephants in the cabinet that month. There weren't a lot of fuckers, not of the evil sort. Fifteen lips on the back porch are better than no eyes. Which is what Adam has.

Razors were a part of us, too. That stem-cell assertion. Adam got hit in the head with a microphone stand. That's what happens to the blind in this nation.

Like a hair stuck beneath a piece of scotch tape, the Whore was pregnant with suspicions. She was lost in a pile of teenage pajamas, each of which had been double-dipped in sperm and ice cream to assure their extra large putrilage benefit factor. I mean, monkey grease? We can satisfactualize context, but a confession in the US is like wearing a dress. Marble centipedes in the bathroom mirror. The Whore thought she'd find abortion tablets in there, but all she found was someone else's collection. Why do these teenage boys collect things? As though cataloguing those bits of life with memoryless guarantees could protect from those objects' self-sure demise. Can't you sniff the expiration date on your soul, the Whore had to ask herself. She didn't know which golden nugget contained the correct answer.

If you want healthy dry skin, you're gonna have to ask me to abandon you right after this, Peter whispered to Arnold.

Lots of buttfuckery had gone down in that islet of a House, yet no one knew. Not even those who had participated. That's because they had all been sanded down, their respective beings. Something so funky about being trapped. The vicious verb that goes into defining one's opposite.

Don't jack off on my ego, you nitwit, I'll sew you into the carpeting and then spill coca cola classic on your lackluster incarnate till the wheat sprouts out of your harried ambivalence. Retardation in the west coast blues scene.

Taylor: spun into the third-rate ego. Not an enviable place to be. And to think, he had come on board to save them all! Now he's been reduced to the status of mere commentary. It's always hard to play the angel when your cheesed genitals are ensnared in a satanic birdcage. People are thinking about it, they are.

Out-on-the-street twink wants to be let inside. The juiceless anarchist waifer was burning in the kitchen. When he sees himself, he thinks of someone else. A lot of diagnostic faggots have this problem. They were in the wrong jail, the new ones. Taylor was hiding in the laundry. We're not capitalists in the traditional sense. There is always something wrong with something.

Taylor had gotten so wayward, Zach had to come in the laundry room and give him new instructions. He was the type of person who could fart on cue, even without being told what to do. There were a bunch of flies stuck to a piece of scotch tape.

Taylor's head emerged from the laundry pile. What is healthy is the vibration that knows it is lost. When nothing happens, a lesbian. Her teeth form pubescent wandering, the sanitized shirking of form—how distant it all can be! Writing on the bottom of my foot, I come alive. How narrow it all is, it all can be...

Penis is the window, Adam said, poignantly.

Taylor gave Zach a squirrel necklace. Everyone cried. Is it time for us all to go to hell yet? A fish sandwich would be nice.

Adam: Peanut butter n' jelly, your mother. The thereafter, please.

God's filthy slut came into the kitchen like she hadn't a clue. And then she did. And then she didn't once again. This trying, life took so much out of her, then put it back in again. It was a lot like visiting Cleveland the summer of your senior year. Too many battles and the yearning to escape them all simultaneously.

The knife was leaking all over her. She called out Adam's name, defenseless; but she was already inside of Adam. Adam recalled he was banned from home for punching his porn star mother in the schnozzola and calling her a shit-eating witch. Now he had no place to go back to. Every place is the same. Do you want to buy your way out of that zit? Shut up, Peter.

Lukas and Adam were in the kitchen, plotting revolution in the hairways. I'll have the scrambled legs without bacon. They're going all over the place, happily, those scrunched-up bugs that fly sideways. Peter plots a revolution all by himself, it is a grand spectacular, it is a revolution that has been commissioned by god (Taylor), the parrot flies in the window and lands on his left shoulder, everything we are leaning towards is truly justified.

Sanctification? Get away from here o lord. It all started out innocent enough, but to be a teenager for all time? Arnold had a slight problem with that, this never growing past the fears that gnaw you, that edge you on towards an even darker spot on the map. The music in his ears told him which variables should be trusted and in what order. He's playing the drums now in the kitchen, but there is no rhythmic semblance to what he bangs out; just the mayhem of speed and indifference. This is so shocking to the others, or at least those who haven't been conditioned to germinate false ideals. A helicopter flew over the house, causing Zach to run out into the front yard screaming with a knife in his hand and cut the pig's throat.

It's a reminder, isn't it, to be proper most of the time. The way you examine my livestock makes me nervous itch. Becoming mineral was Adam's project. He had it all sketched out on the side of a lamp. All he needed was one more defeatist notion to complete the etching. Down a proper alleyway to become a livid burden once again.

Let's kill the president take a shit on its corpse.

Gone is the lunar tide that was once upon us, guiding this mission through motel rooms vast and 'blong. Owner violation calls the cops on chance, arrive arrive, your movementary sediment is blowing. One-armed sailor is what Zach once thought of becoming. If we could swordfight the air, we might win a trip to the outer european. Days when pirates were upon us, and thus we became, all unevenly and at most.

Humbled by the train wreck that had just occurred in the lower reaches of his fibula, Adam waited. The television had a crack in it roughly the shape of an X. It's because of all that porno mayhem that we had seethed out earlier as a means of primal expression. Allegory's fade into orificial layers; scotch tape scissor hope to best friend's forehead. Adam has so many friends, I think he'll die. Ferretsquidowl flies past us and Lukas is forced to scream out oh shit.

What do those specs smell like, are you sniffing Jesus? We couldn't rastify your transmissive overlode if you swallowed. That's what truth burned like: saver. You caught on once you finished the contemplation. Anarchist savors completion. (Not deem me out sexual to be a raw night competition.)

Brief disturbance serves as a sort of interlude, the last two segments of character study. Elicited Adam and Arnold to re-compete in the first name game. Whore be the judge; deadlier than on a blanket.

All I want is the human race to suck me satisfied, said the Whore aloud to all her boyfriends. The Suiciders wouldn't listen. They had revolution on their brain cells. The Whore used a cloth napkin to wipe it off. I want to tie a bomb to my jockstrap and go into the gym like that. That's one way of terminating a dryspell.

The revolution must be deep-fried, said Lukas plaintively. Once you can handle the onions, you can tackle the smell. Taste is always tertiary to ambition. The second item long forgotten.

My brain is an experienced maverick to not be tasted, Zach asserts. Oh baby I love your loveless authority. Dangle the figures deeper into my havenish court. That last one was the Whore's sentience.

The authority figure gives me a backrub. Quit hiding.

To challenge the equinox. Gay? We are all loving winds past distraction. Horny, yet functional. I love how he's in Bermuda this time of year, Pete whispers to Arnold. But Arnold is Matthew's lover, cries Adam. Lukas and Peter don't know each other.

The Whore's asshole grew a flower. She asked the abortionist to pick it. The abortionist does not want to destroy nature.

These are all authorities we have to listen to. Shifty elephants in need of relief. That's what the organizers seemed to resemble. That whore's mohawk must've really been about something.

A true antichrist always has hair.

Eat my psychologist, fuckface.

Fascist dingdong? Or alliterative wingwong? Hold a shield to the hero and ding my thong. A fuck is the only earthliness; forget about saving. Tentative apples reaching up to the ceiling. My primordial is so fit it is ready to be trimmed. Curly hair is so me, it's not even worth it to fire up the gas oven. But then we're torn apart—thorns are flying high. We can't go too deep in the shade without drowning. We've got it all pre-arranged. Which is to say…justified.

Risky blissness! Thank all the fuckwads that once competed to fill your lifestyle up. That way you will know which trophy to award and why. In the specific order of my transmission, I smell you too. The thought trifles away at Lukas's sunburn, he is out of bounds, the limit. We're thinking we can be on top of that void. That's when we decided to call a meeting.

The Whore must triumph over us as we speak our language's last form. Fascist dingdong could emerge triumphant, where would that take us. The dickvoid is abounding, the street. I am not that type of avoider. I know someone else. As soon as the corporate bubble popped, your face got lost. The smog inside my grandma is teaching me a lesson. The bland eyeballs that chase after. The dog cries when he is not on fire.

The throat spider crawled into Adam's mind. Sharpening the transcendental buttplug, Matthew fell in. Peter came over to think about something. The flow of oxygen sounds pretty.

Arnold, are you up to your oral hijinks again?

No one can save us, we are only mustard in a tube. The fanaticism of daisies outside the forest. I love your racist hairstyle Adam, did you download that or get it for free?

When someone perpetuates their existential teenagehood through fire, all sorts of motherfuckerdom gets sprouted into the faceless jaw zone. Whoever owns a mattress can come over right now. That's the announcement Zach made through the intercom at the top of the stairs. Suddenly the whole neighborhood was down in their basement. That's when they turned the fire hose on.

A whole history of history getting drowned. Soapbox radiance, the preacher everyone voted for. Our high commanders are shitting themselves everytime they hear our voices broadcast through the broken television set they keep for company. All danger has been annihilated; this common world. Perpetuity has a gasmask on. Give me more of your three-dollar bills please. I want a new exception.

The other day I went over to Christ's house in order to have a problem. Rapid individuals came to serenade me. This is Zach speaking. You need a truth serum. Why I never have time to unvague what I'm going for. The elasticized apple too much to gain.

Last winter Lukas went out the window. He thought it was too dangerous to come back inside, so he lived on the rooftop for the rest of the season, only a color TV to keep him warm. Once he had figured out a way inside the TV, he could re-enter the living room, where Zach was holding court over the local youth movement.

Zach and Lukas and Adam and Arnold are starting a breakaway faction, a sort of rock n' roll subcommando unit, with young children smashing vases against the neighbors' mailboxes. All this will happen in time, Zach keeps telling them. He doesn't tell the children that they will grow up one day to become teenagers just like us. He doesn't want to spoil the surprise, the longing. Besides, what we know is the thing that we will never become best. The hardness of the mattress is what matters, not how much straw you stuff it with.

CHAPTER 22

Lukas **disappears**
before the **narrative** even gets a
chance **to finish.**

A funeral without a **corpse.**
Adam wrote this.

Then one day Lukas disappeared! (Was it the White Nothing?) Oh my fuck, what will we do in this narrative without him, I'm gonna cry.

They all were just walking down the street one day in a city that resembled New Orleans without the whores when all of a sudden he just sparked and then he was gone, poor Lukas.

Arnold's such an interesting person. He insulted me one time. It felt so good to be recognized in public back then. See, we're in this really famous rock band. You should come see us play sometime.

A flower holds sway, the power of gray. Mute amphibian on a leash, being walked by Zach and Taylor. They resemble a gay couple even though they don't know what they are. They are seeking. Their amphibian meant as a response to Jesus, a provocation. A Lukas substitute like any other. Will they name their amphibian Lukas or Jesus? It will be a name like any other.

The reality substitute has got me on his farm. I don't want to be a tropical vietnamese woman anymore. I only want to know what fits and what's wrong with her. Whorish nightmare can be viewed from in-between the curtains, a special phase that reveals itself lightly. So much feeling was poured out going down that road. Trapped in the other american city, no one can inhale the freedom much longer. They are seeing ghosts, they are being other than themselves somehow. Arnold is there to provide a human mirror.

Why is Arnold interesting, Lukas says.

Lukas isn't there anymore.

Perhaps that is merely Zach's amphibian talking then.

Quit screwing up the narrative, dingus, Adam interjects, I'm trying to write this one all on my own. That's all you ever do Adam that's why we can't seem to get anywhere. At least we are moving, Peter says.

The thunder is all over us, it is a storm. It is a ghost of letting-go, a season. There is no highness we might subscribe to. The otherness that delineates this particular strata of terrain melts in front of the Whore's mound. A license to fall apart can only be granted to the sealless ones among us. What can't be fought we can at least bite through. There is no teenage mother called god.

Are you okay, love, get off the spider. Marc's erection was huge. He didn't have much of an answer. It's okay when you see it in the toilet. That fandanglement floating there. My operative device, it can surely be transcendent. It makes me laugh to hear my euthanasia like that. Global scattering of forces is something that wears us down, we are there so lightly, it is like we are twins for our own selves. The raped forces among us are whispering Lukas's name as a mourning symbol, pride. Enlightenment scattered in only one direction. That's the force we're framing right about now.

Feral forces oh the waves. Lukas was never the leader of our army. We have to move on, remember his spark. To the dayness and the sun, the leanings of our putrid master, he was always the One. And although we might never find a better guitar player, we can at least embrace what we have left of him, his capillaries. A question: What does wordless do when we run after it? Smeared ambitions on the radar, a truth tunnel to bespoke the fly. Gunning down to the humanlity, crossed wires perhaps cause a human life. To be reborn into situationlessness. What my whole personality just changed it was like a shotgun before. Waves are upon us, we did it all.

Arnold provides us with a new definition of death let's jump right in. He's such an interesting person. He keeps all our bandit fans away from us. They might want to crush us in this hour of mourning. The fans just don't understand. They can't understand our teenage band. Our band with four hands. An all-man band. We are rich and we are thin. You cannot see us, we stretch our skin. We are one and we're the same. We're the Suiciders, that's our game.

Here comes a knife again inside the silence. Zach had to go off and recuperate in the other america, the wilderness portion of it. We decided to remain behind in the other america's version of New Orleans (never the same). The Whore went on down there with us, she had a weapon. Saviors are something I once thought about.

A wave came and washed it all away, this city, the setting for our new music video. I can abide by the silence, but only when I have crabs. The meat inside the forecast, that was holy as doubt's spleen. Well-endowed the youthful pirate who just creamed on my breakfast. Adam was starting to fade. He didn't want to have black hair no more, he was so depressed, he didn't know what he was doing that season. A realm like any other. But with Zach's absence piled onto Lukas's, there were no leaders to guide us through the sewer that late chinese autumn.

Here comes my goddamn. It hurts soon, it's true. Don't angst on my spiderweb, that's meant to be Adam's primal intention! Correct symbology is never correct. Caustic delineation might lead us waywards. The Whore has a monologue.

Gather round, pet spiders, so I can inform you all of my flipfloppy harelippery. Here comes a lesson of my derangement. I need all of your left foot socks in a pile before me right here. I will name each and every one of them, and see if that name corresponds to your unflinching attribute span. I'm okay, the satellite's awake, here wanna hunt my trophy? I'm in the business of responding. You are the time, and here I am living. Oh, I'm a humorous webcam, aren't I. You can laugh, but you'll never have half the answers I just vomited up. They're in my throat, I'm downtown. You're the last intention I ever thought about burning. Here, try not to channel someone else's voice for a minute. You can't do it, can you? The holes in the garden are just unfair. Diarrhea from the mouth of an angel. Spaniards in the other america? Fuck that—wasted on the wafer. We know how it burns. We are medicinal ourselves. Living it up, my goddamn. We can't go much higher than the self-holocaust's limitations. Primordial: that's a bucket of fire. My anti-throat device. You just thought of yourself as an organization. No can smell. I still don't know why you're going after me. I was just on my way to salvationland, looking for the grand pick-up. Suddenly I was after. What is it? A delectability? Sinus rays the material infection? Grant suicide lobbyist the ultimate discourse, that which you are seeking. C'mon kids, we don't need another virus to be deployed at the wrong hour. We are leaning towards the desert, we shriek in our own underwear. Isn't it amazing? We are ready for the cement truck to fall on us. To be thusly annihilated is the only allegory. Peace on a plane. OMG, here comes Florida.

When the Whore had finished with her metaphor, she farted. A crystal ball came out of her orifice, the christmas carollers on the doorstep. I can't believe what you just put down in front my eyeball, she said. I mean I'm strong, but you aren't there.

The sun did its thing all over her eyes.

Don't let wordless in, she'll never leave. Wordless is a whore with no eyebrows. She has a stunning set of sideburns instead.

The other night before Lukas disappeared he called out to my vision in a dream, Adam said. Even though I ain't got no eyeballs don't mean that the vision doesn't melt inside me every time I go to take a pee. Now my momentum's in the vacuum cleaner. Are you out past Sunday? Where's my dog.

I'm no-name, pleased to be embarrassed by you. The damn sexiness of dawn just got all over my shirt. You play the spiral warp rush, but you don't really understand how to end it. Dicksucker choreography. You might not be as shaved as you think.

I think there is only one way we can let gesture win, and that is if it radiates. We can't all be from China around here no more.

Colonize all boundaries, the other america is like a whale. So let geography be the principle. We are forever undivided. Arnold lost his heartache in someone else's toilet. The river runs with abandon, we are through with being here. The success rate among mexicans varies. Being artless has its borders also.

Lukas just got on the radio, I heard his voice. Maybe he's not such a spark after all. If his voice still remains, there is nothing worth diving for. Sometimes just a virulent strain of protein, always arriving. Arnold has a conflict.

Down in the ocean, we weren't a friendly version of New Orleans' otherness. Bondage is on the other side of the city. The messiness of earthtone days.

Zach came back all black and brown. He couldn't wear a frown. He kept falling down. Just like in that other novel. The feelings were all the same. He needed a fruitbox to stand on and say his peace. Now there are children chasing after him. At least it wasn't a dog.

Lukas was afraid of dogs, and perhaps that is why he had to go away. Arnold's such an interesting person. We won't take the time to investigate him, there are too many others. Marc is a narrative. The eagle's sorry.

My indifference is already straining you. A too-tight mantel-piece. Don't be on top of dryness. You're so subcultural. Matthew is a monkey, the hole in one.

Matthew goes on his webcam in order to feel something. True emotion the turkish authentical, okay? It's not goddamn Spain, it's the other america.

Farting his livelihood, he won a second trophy.

I don't know what happened, I'm a slave, said Peter.

Does the goddamn carpenter have a stake in this? He's always channeling the wrong estrogen. And Arnold always thought a carpenter was a person who fixed carpets. Thus assuming a position of religious insolence.

I love the drag queen a force of nature. Adam said the others. He can't admit. Hold on, he's pulling out a quotation. My hair hurts.

Farrah Fawcett gays having abortions all over each other's eyeballs; have we really been reduced to this? Where is my fruit livelihood? New theory of the proper name = slur. Says Adam.

She wasn't the type of nun you wanted to shit on. The onely ones, the banquet bitch. Whore needs a break from this episode. Adam's throat spider inside her. Adam keeps calling out, wanting to be led. Even further other americas will emerge from this one. Wet shadow leaves its stain across the ceiling. Bloodless arms collaborate in congealing. My america, your putrid vestibules. Supernal doubters shout down my butthole ambivalence.

The truth is a retard, says Marc. He is not a character. Adam's porn star mother is sad. She just ate some beef. Now she feels better again. The story's over. You can all go home now and jerk off on your favorite cop's face. People are more likely to own something when they don't show it.

Someone's earhole violated. An account of where Zach was when the vacation occurred—what you never get in the sitcom. Well-sat upon annihilation? Who's the chimney thief among us. Peter wants to go back to the house. There, things will be sacred once again. No, we can never go back there, not for the rest of this goddamn narrative. Things cannot be achieved. They can only be commanded. The outer dictator is joyful joyful. A teenage heart attack.

I don't know where this fucked place-name is. I misplaced it, misnamed it also. That double negates it, and thus asserts something.

Peter got a job being himself today in some other way. That's a rule broken: no one from the Suiciders is allowed to get a proper job. That sort of ambition is heavily frowned upon. Maybe not heavily—it depends on who's doing the frowning. Still, we're ready. Taylor wants to excommunicate. But Taylor is a new member, one chosen by our vacationing leader. This is not a sitcom, it's a lifestyle, okay?

The studio audience laughs. The audience doesn't know what it is. That's its problem. It has to remain an it, unpersonified. The blatancy of my undoubted charms. It becomes a given, the wax of the sea. Keeping it broken in the other america.

The White Nothing was behind him. Don't let it chase you down the staircase, Lukas. All your thoughts will come out, it won't be pretty. But Lukas, he was standard. He had black hair like the rest of us, all his dreams were shattered vinyl. To get back up on top, he had to let it all in. That obliterative night immer allowed to stalk us. The sordid fires that gives us reason. To impel movement. The never enough to be true. Peter and Matthew. Adam. No more Lukas. Taylor and Matthew and Arnold. Arnold and Marc. Marc is not a character. Zach and Taylor and Adam. Matthew and Arnold and Peter. Matthew and the Whore. The Whore has her variables also. Matthew and Arnold and Adam. Adam and Peter. Matthew and Zach. Zach and Adam. Marc.

Thus it was that the winds blew us all down. We didn't want to be glued to the ceiling any longer. Someone else had to let us in through the back window.

CHAPTER 23

The Suiciders
hide in an
Artist's studio
in the other america's
version of New Orleans.
Fear of the present.

B ut distance makes caricatures of us all.

They had formed a suicide pact as children cos children do such things. That doesn't mean they were bad people. I know it would be illegal to kill myself. I wanna kill Adam instead.

Retards are another species. The boys went into hiding. They had to escape the White Nothing, which had eaten Lukas, not to mention the Police that was after them all. The Police is always there, even when we don't want it to be. To be on top of one another only in time. The present's gayness has a purple hat on. I am looking forward to the distant evasion.

They were no longer in the house doing something; they were in someone else's house now. Doing something. They had had to get away. Away away to the other america's New Orleans.

There the heat threatened to burn what was left of their minds. Their tired minds, tired from too much sleeping.

In their hiding place, Adam writes a new song. Institutions are fun things. Zach wants to have an advantage. He is singing the dirt ball song. The molester. Is Taylor's mom after us too? I don't want to go over that bridge again. Standing inside the mindball is fun, too. It's when we re-trample the territory that my nerves get snagged.

Teenage regrets, they don't last long. The rope of time proves strong enough to hang yourself with. Don't worry. Looking back, it's the little things that'll matter least. Others delineate your memory for you. The first time you jerked off, that pillow between your legs, you wouldn't even remember the pattern. Whether it was your right hand or your left. All those objects, those toys from your childhood that you'd outgrown, how you'd shove them up your ass in order to heighten the orgasm. Or the stuffed animal you cut a hole in the side of, until it got too moldy you had to throw it out.

The heretic retard in the bart simpson t-shirt is the one who led them to their new hide-out. He had a lot to say, you just had to pay him a quarter and it was there. He wasn't the type to go shooting up his high school with a machine gun. There were others for that duty.

No one knew where the perverted Whore had run off to. She must have found a sudden purpose for her existence. She'll be back later, said Adam. How will she find us. She always deciphers the trail.

Blow your mind all out of proportion.

In the hiding place, there was an artist. It was his basement. We didn't want to use it, his materials. We just had to be there until the fuzz evaporated. Who knew when that would be. I'm not a priest, I can't predict things. I just have a swell tan. So be it. Peter has a tube of vaseline.

Eat my hole Adam.

Adam can't fuck no more he went blind. Peter is here to satisfy you until the cop cravings go away. The Artist was suspicious. He didn't want them being in his atelier, being all over his atelier. He had an important art to make, and the deadline was yesteryear. Matthew got excited. Finally we're around someone doing something important. Lukas wasn't there.

I remember my own teenage years, being surrounded by disease. It was the city of someone else's dream, I had my tongue out all the time, trying to tell the temperature. There weren't any gods to tell me what to do, it was so sad. I'm not much of a man, but neither is your ego. The scientologist farted. Matthew and Adam.

The question is can all abstain from touching one another while we are in hiding. Such cramped quarters. This is no longer a decade devoted to revolutionary causes; no one fucks. It's okay, we can be ashamed together. Guys.

Send the Artist to the supermarket. Guys. I want some food. Guys. Make him buy us beer. Guys. We can all pretend to like each other. Guys. Be friends with me. Guys. I'm going to import a hairdresser. Guys.

Adam is all over the place this time of year. I think it's because he has something to say. Something to say about the state of the world today. Literature happens when you comb your hair. I am not suicidal enough to care.

Don't let the Whore invade our hide-out. Being suicidal is so much fun. We have to meditate now. We aren't punk rockers. We like the sun. Peter says the ceiling is too low here. Don't describe our circumstances please, I don't want the outside world to know about it.

The Artist told us to go away. Zach threatened him with a shotgun. He decided to let us stay.

Sometimes circumstances lead you somewhere. I don't want to be challenged. Matthew's name was Marc all of a sudden. The confusion. Scrapped centimeters, the legion of holelessness. The ferret went into the forest. We don't want to go back to that chapter right now. The writing of it was so easy. We want to be challenged by our listlessness. This is group endeavor. Guys. You don't understand?

Arnold slept on the wrong side of his face last night. Woke up all wrong. His insides were out. Okay, man? No. Certain limitations are never demented, they are only a trophy to be awarded to the biggest loser among us. The one who lasts the longest. I've eaten narratives that taste worse than this. You don't want to go on about the Outsiders. This is the goddamn Suiciders.

Here's some blood for you to munch on, salvation. The salvation army whore won't be coming over. She found another satellite to chase after. Her burns were all real; covered by hairs. Oh, that was so devilish! You licked me too? Adam is using the Artist's art supplies.

No one here is allowed to create any masterpieces, Zach says, not while we're in residence. The Artist had no one to go home to. He only had the bathroom sink. It hadn't been cleaned in a long while. That's okay, we didn't want to use it for anything except urine disposal. I went out in the hallway to use the payphone to call the Whore.

She had a chinese appetite most couldn't furnish. Sunburned shitless, she didn't want a man. She couldn't talk long on the phone or else she'd melt the plastic. A dirty third-rate hunger announced through the receiver.

I like how you're not a molecule. I want to fuck you in Kenya. I like how you're not illusive. The bottom drowners take it all out on stone. What the second-rate satellite furnishes is too much hope to vibrate by. Liquor-stained piss crick.

A meditative moment, run over my face please. I really like the smell of you when you're doing the slapdance. Come over to my house and bleed me a miracle.

Adam's in the corner burying himself in a pile of sand bags. He's blind, he doesn't know what he's doing, he thinks it's the salt of the earth. Presidential liar drinks too many juices. I tasted the salt ones, too. You can't be brave when you're high on nitrous.

It hurts when you flow from me. This is a distant assertion made too fast. We were sitting in a room all of a sudden, describe this. How we found this situationality I'll never know. Matthew has so many friends. Your eyeballs screw me. Adam's math was absence. He was tired. When you have no eyes, you never know when you're asleep.

It's okay to be okay today. Some will screw; some will lose. Some will be okay and that's okay too. The news. Are we on it yet? I don't have a victim. Taylor's cousin Kelli. She wanted us to stay in the woods. Those black things were haunted. The White Nothing stares.

I just shot your mom in the face. I hope it's okay. Zach gets a kick out of terrorizing the Artist, I don't know why. Taylor has to calm him down. Taylor understands Zach in ways none of us can straddle. The grammar police is here to divide.

Police is always singular, never plural. That's the only way you can understand the force. The grammar has to have an abortion before you can file your appeal. No one can love anyone from a distance anymore, the internet has corroded. I love your shit in the ghetto. Climb the scales. The number twenty-five.

Ten dollars, ten dollars. That's all the artist wants, and then we can stay. The Suiciders have no money. They don't believe in it. Can't we make you a new dishrag? The old one has paint all over it. I want to fornicate the orangutan.

The space next door to the Artist's studio was being occupied by a group of militant transsexual orthodontists. None of your jokes are allowed to be funny, Taylor says. (He was speaking for Zach just then.) Ride the escalator down the hill. A chipmunk dances on the laundry room floor.

I just looked at my lips in the mirror. I was feeling constrained by my own expectations. Zach and Adam prepare to die. They have to write out the instructions, it is so complicated.

Ten dollars became twenty. Twenty became four. We were all asleep in a pile on the floor. None of us were naked. We had no need to be, as of yet. Everyone else thought of excuses, I was nearly annihilated.

My image of god is as a big giant fish tank, only floating. An initial floating shit in the center of it, and now I have a pet monkey. Body so sensual. (Sensual is not actually a word.)

Sometimes the world knows things. You have to be in Ethiopia to understand it. Just like life, resolution is something that gets imposed. Don't lick it, the flames are rare. The Police is everywhere. Zach, stop being so paranoid. You're our leader, don't you remember?

Did something meow that was just inside me? When people become verbs, they often dye their hair. I have an important announcement to make: I'd like fish sticks for dinner this evening.

But the Whore was off dryhumping with another, an other that must remain nameless here, for he was the presidential election. Violating an owl through the window. Eat my intestinoids, bitch. The mushroom sandwich tastes suspiciously like morning.

Omigod, it feels so good, the satellite. The nun with the tumor on her tit really knew how to grow tomatoes. I really wanna thank you for being so satisfactual in your diseased exchanges with me. There was a lot of mummification to subsist on in those years, and you really broke it through. We're never very waxy when desire is leading us somewhere. We identify more with the apes than we do the paradoxes.

Oh, here comes the sun, I think I'll open the window, I forgot there wasn't one?

Lonely bikeriders get it for free. I'm talking that seatless affect. Don't shave my anticipation off that sandwich! Whichever reich you're talking about, I only want the screwdriver to lift me out of it.

I'm about you also, it's true. This failure.

Somewhere it's bleeding. Time. You have to know to count the others. They don't want you. They are merely asserting. The smiles fade. You're going to go away. The feeling's been asserted. We're entering the artwork. This meditative silence that just got stabbed. Journalistic faghag always narrates. The southern loss far afield.

Hear me speak the goddamn. Zach's in the Artist's kitchen, trying to bake his own left arm. He just wants to know how it'll feel. Adam's saying I'm glad we accomplished that, really. Blasted scale can't hold me in. Can't hold truth, either.

Well I like to do the slapdance, he said through the computer camera, the slapdance routine. Head up on the eel, motherfucker!

Then he made an Adamlike squeak into a tape recorder and played it right back for all of us. It was a moment described.

Are you doing anymore devotional dong layers? Finally to be found makes up for coming after. Fell down uncoded, unitary bra stain. I am better than most things that moan. Sharper in the desert really, the unbridled pay phone.

You don't know what love is (until you've sat on my face and cried). I hate almost everything.

Oh hormony, let me lick yr catheterous existence. I'm no snatch, I'm just burning. My face on that cross? No way. I won't leave you unattended.

It was a whale of a day when spring finally came they were all indoors. It was a shrine, the lesbian. Here I'm making a new painting, wanna come up to my attic?

Said Adam to the Artist.

Power walkers usually armed with grenades. We couldn't watch. Juiceless in the enterprise, aqua marinelife to feel all right. Arnold's sentiment, we're going after. Around the riverscape, no one meant to foliate.

Joggers.

The nod to sensation. I've forgotten which observance. Matthew came upon the others writing. Once is all the same.

Put myself in a vulnerable spot your head stance upside down. Why bother reaching out the others cannot catch you there. Flowery escapades, you wrote the wrong letter. I don't want the townscape to give birth once again, said the Artist. He was talking to nobody.

Throw my hairs in the oven; you're a philosopher? Lukas never thought the bottle would float. Now I'm a character. At least the stuffing could be honest. If only we weren't all truly away.

Adam's sad. It makes him calm to feel the radiation. There is fish in his salad. He is flexible enough to care.

Taylor's mom outside our hideout. The goddamn cunt has teamed up with Police. We're really not so vagary like. Police is a machine our nails; goddamn carnival barkers alliance. Was it the retard that showed us the hideout that showed them/it? A barking animal is its siren. Police doesn't know our legacy. Police is going to be put inside the dungeon, the dungeon of our fears. Zach is talking through a walkie-talkie. He doesn't want to communicate. Adam's thickly saying something. Police is gonna die.

We're all loaded up, we've got guns too y'know. We're about to do some hardcore civic damage to your environment, if you don't watch out. This is not a lawless atmosphere; we've written our own. Taylor stuck his head outside the window to spit on the canal. Cuntmother certainly isn't so virtuous as we once thought. Dreams're finagled. It was your cousin Kelli who told us Taylor don't blame Police it's only trying to be our friend?

Police emerges through the thick haze of the White Nothing. A siren in a cloud. Police Christ. We've got a blind one in here. Go ahead, rub yr guns all over my body. The Artist shows them his master's degree.

You're so amazing, you're an amazonian.

Don't police my black desire, bitch. We're gonna suicide ourselves if we have to take this entire world with us. The world we'd be doing it a favor anyhow. There are no modern forms of worship. A cafeteria worker's hairnet is a nice amusement from time to time. The Artist was in the kitchen frying noodles. I feel like eating a chocolate bunny.

Peter's so afraid of becoming too bisexual to speak. And so he set off the alarm in the atelier. Police busted in and we shot its butthole dead. Now it's time to get out of the storyline. Zach doesn't want superheroes to predominate. As soon as that happens, we'll all be doing jumping jacks on Uranus. The cows have been made love to. The color orange is black. Police is not a force it is an entity. Police is not an entity it is a force.

Anyway you take a bath is a good way, Peter told Arnold. Arnold was afraid of dying. It's okay Arnold just get rid of all psychology. I'm feeling the need to be quoted. Oh, leather operator, you are doing this to yourself. Zach was still wallowing around when he shoved the Artist's head in the frying pan and blew a whistle. I'm not a monster I'm just a celebrator. Where has the day gone? You pretty much just had a baby just then didn't you. Militant sasquatch just sat on my favorite name. Humans want breathing time of their own to navigate.

I can be the leaders of youths lost and brown.

Please stop having an identity on me. Yes we're awake also.

Looking at pictures from my friends' lives, I often wonder about them. Going inside the cradle, yes, you're lonely. Police is outside to tell us all our fears. I hope on an individual basis. I want to be violated in the most unique fashion imaginable. Something about medieval bra stains.

I took Marc (this was Matthew's name all of a sudden) out of the water to explain something to him. Marc bit me. I know this was a sign. It was time for our teen suicide pact to become real.

CHAPTER 24

The names.

I remember all of the words to our teen suicide pact. I fucking
shake when I hear them read out loud again cos it's the only
bible I ever knew. Marc goes down on Arnold one more time.
Arnold and Matthew groan in pain. Marc's cock is so huge.
Then we switched and I fucked Arnold while Matt fucked
Adam. I put some grease all over his Adam's Apple and sat on it.
His entire neck disappeared up my ass. I'm female.

Brody jacks his big fat meatbone while Adam videotapes.
Adam gets a hard-on, which is fellated by Samuel. Samuel is getting fucked by Lukas. Matthew and Peter fuck in the corner.
Arnold sits on Zach's erect member. The bondage earthworm
burns some TP. Brody smokes a cigarette as he strokes Arnold's
cock. This is the end of days. Fabricated lilacs kicking back.
Adam likes to touch the magic wand while he's asleep. Robert is
on the sidewalk. He groans in his lapse of memory as he make
poopoo on his geriatricistic fucktard.

Peter's dick is bigger than a car. The Whore farts on the face
of god. Then she turns around and rides god reverse cowgirl
style. Don't let any gods younger than me fuck me. She whispers

to the other boys in the gangbang. She wants to be told a story while she's being violated.

A dog fucks a whore on live webcam. The teenagers have all been reduced to mere status symbols. Eat my legendary granola on time tonight. Taylor has his face in the dogbowl as the whore fucks him with a strap-on from behind, marketing viral all the while.

Lukas holds a lit match to Adam's urethra as Zach ducttapes his asshole shut. The priest shaves off all his asshair and shoves a fire hose up his daughter's snatch, then blasts her wide open. Lukas jacks off apelike on Adam's face. The violated rugby player shoots his own mother in the mouth with a beebee gun and rapes her ass. A midget comes out of the alleyway with a sword and stabs the Whore in the face while she's sucking Adam. Lukas's humungous balls tremble as Zach hungrily tosses his salad, then adds a creamy white dressing to it.

Sallie Mae gets pounded doggy-style by Peter, while Arnold videotapes with a camcorder from a previous decade. Adam's mother in the other other america is seduced by a jackhammer. The Pope shits on Lukas's hairstyle, a soviet nun has to clean it off. Frying Pan Jesus comes in and smacks Zach's bulbous buttcheeks real real hard, he swats him away and continues burrowing his way into the midget's membrane.

A geography of gyrations gets masturbated upon, the Whore's trophy. Taylor became the latest gangbang phenomenon overnight when he was ejected from the bukkake raid. Seventeen owls flew into Peter's new gender, his sex change fell right off into his neighbor's soup. Tony did Arnold the way one man should always do another, if he wants to prove that his hole still contains something.

Sam sprayed his jizz all over the flowery wallpaper, Adam screamed hello. Jack sat on Adam's face and a postcard fell out of his vagina. Peter moans as she shoves the Pope's dildo up his ass. As he's doing that, Susan comes and shaves around the hole. Jake wears a leather jockstrap and is joyful. Lizard comes and licks the filth off his right heel.

Elizabeth wears a blindfold and is tied to a chair. She wants all the men with vowels in their first names to come take advantage of her nasal passage with their balkan meat swords. Meanwhile, Arnold masturbates with a leather bra beneath his sac. Arnold sucks Adam's dick while fucking Zach, who is bent over the washing machine reading a paperback novel. No one wears a necklace.

Arnold then inserts his male member into Zach's eager hungry sugarmouth. Arnold sits in a chair and Zach continues to ride like the lonesome cowboy he never was. Arnold gets bored and puts on someone else's glasses. Now he can't see. But that's okay. He never wanted to know anyone's last name to begin with.

Adam cuts a hole in the side of Susan's head and fucks it oh so good. He shoots his purple neon sperm into her and it leaks radioactivity out of her eyeballs. Susan moans with a satisfaction she has never felt before; a freestyle lobotomy was her ultimate fantasy, and now it is coming so true, just as Arnold is cumming in Amanda's face. Lukas can't get enough of Sean's blue collar cock. He wants to dress up in a fur coat and get his hepatitis C ass fisted by a sympathetic pony.

Sam removes his underwear and sticks it up Zach's ego. Taylor is strung up on the magazine rack, wailing, as the Whore removes potatoes from her pussy and pummels him in the face from across the room. He wants to get up and leave, but then a horse comes and fucks him. An illiterate moron with a broken cock comes over to say hello. An arabic teenager shits on the bible and makes Matthew eat it all up. Before he gets a chance to finish, Susan comes and dips her lollypop in it, then shoves it up the horse's vag.

A christian deepthroater named Samantha comes and tap-dances on Lukas's face. A ferret runs into her twat and screams. A satanic jailbird named Tom wears a cockring. He chokes on a lollypop while Samantha sucks him dry.

Peter cuts Arnold's balls off and feeds them to Jesus H. Christ, a muslim convert. Arnold rips Tom wide open and wears a cowboy hat to prove it. Lukas fucks so bad Samantha has to laugh at him while he tries to do it. A fat gay hindu comes and sings.

Camera clicks away as Matthew chokes down on someone else's juices. The Whore's nostrils are wide open. A homeless man wanders in and decides to join in on the fun; he violates Fannie Mae in the crudest way possible, then serenades her with a one hit wonder.

Peter chokes on Zach's huge buddhistic boner, pukes beer and mint chocolate chip ice cream up all over it, Adam comes and licks it off.

Fat whore rides a dildo moaning, squeals all over herself and dies. Old man bitchslaps his leatherbound wife, rides the underage boner of Taylor, who is now in a wheelchair. Freddie Mac speaks a foreign language while he barebacks Zach. Zach's hole is so tender, he almost said no.

No is a word the dirty whore just doesn't understand. She doesn't have to; she never had a name. She takes three cocks at once in her pus-filled crevice, smoking a cigarette all the while like she's taking her Monday morning dump.

Taylor shits on his stepsister's grandma, illegitimate by a year. Zach gets married to his cousin in a caravan gypsy ceremony that few others are willing to attend clothed. Lukas takes his pants down and whips Peter in the face with his hot and ready pistol stick. The mexican transvestite's cock is ready to spew smoke.

Fat fuck parrot blows over and inhales the wrong system. The teenage parasite chokes on someone's eyeball. Pretty soon it will all be over, Zach tells Taylor, fucking. I can't wait till we get to mutilate each other again, Lukas tells Adam. The Suiciders are so fierce, I think someone just came. The word *over* in capital letters.

Freddie Mac and Robert come and fill each of Adam's eye-sockets with their meat thermometers. Adam pukes all over the snatch of the soviet nun, who shouts out so loud a stalin rainbow appears. A chinese nigger named Satan comes out of the Whore's snatch. The wallpaper's drab truth won't allow anyone to sing through the microphone.

An angel's livelihood is yellow and green. Sallie Mae sticks a cucumber up Fannie Mae's jugular gina. Don't believe me when I tell you how much I'm feeling this right now. A gay knows how to sing, he steps into the reality TV and the Artist comes and sodomizes him right away. His hips move up and down the dildonic throng until a wave of circulatory benevolence shoots through his thighs and reaches Jupiter's outer moon. A satanic birdfeeder is there too.

Hung bicycle rider gets his dick sucked on the moon. You're so good, I wanna give it to you much softer. Old person shits on a twelve-year-old girl; she has all the right symptoms to become the next mormon president.

Ching chong shitblockers on the sidewalk. I keep conjuring the zeroness of it all. Audiodative prison matrix is already present. He didn't want to cockblock my antipathy, so he wrote to the senator's daughter instead. She came and whizzed on his wang. She was normally a chocolate fellator, but she could make an exception as far as the denouement went. Jack rolled over and asked Lukas for a cigarette. Can't you see I'm fucking a rhinoceros at this moment. And I thought it was merely a sour dildo brigade.

Stalin's in the soviet nun's cunt. Flowers grew out of her armpit. She didn't know what else to say. And so she had to have an abortion. The abortion's name was Jesus. Now there are too many of them in this novel.

As soon as I put my face beside you, I think you'll have a pretty good idea of what I smell like. These aren't words a nun would typically utter. Then again, she wasn't your typical nun. People seem to get perverted when they're old. I think it has to do with a lack of exercise. Here comes Simon, all ready to slam. He's in the others. The others are in Sam.

Tony is dressed like an alien and fucks his trannie granddad. Sherbet falls out of her primordial butthole. Awareness in the 1990s machine. The solidarity vibrator is used to shave her mustache off. Kristin licks the gonorrhea off the supreme leader's mustache; fat man with a white beard inserts screwdriver into hermaphroditic piss slit; Chopin's Piano Concerto No.1 in E Minor plays.

Lukas secretes Simon's fluids through his ear into the open willing mouth of Peter. Marc groans in destitute satisfaction as he xeroxes his decapitated member. Lucinda slices her clit off and sends it in the mail to the president elect of the united states. Tony cuts his left testicle off and sends it to the president select of the other america. Zach knows something. He is getting nailed.

Matthew barfs lemon yogurt on Susan's gaping vag and a dog comes and licks it all out. Adam's pet spider is sodomized by trannie strap-on warrior. Arnold pays to get re-birthed anally. The Whore ties Lukas to the bed and licks him until her spit runs dry, then dryheaves her way through his urethral cavity. Fat faggot sings aretha while germs are flung at the toxic tornado. Teenage whore rides the gay donkey upside down.

Arnold farts Peter's upside-down cock out of his greaseless manhole. Taylor shoves the entirety of mohammed up him. Sex with a razor? The dog gets tied to the bed, its four legs spread, Susan whips it while she rubs her clit with her ring finger. Peter's father has an anal abortion in front of his mother. Midget chases after a turtle. Zach performs a presidential lap-dance. Someone's lifestyle.

Joyride father is so clean, you can lick between his toes. Kinky beerbottle fellators don't have children. The nun eats satan's presidential asshole.

Pakistani zionist farm laborer ejaculates all over the Pope's transmission. A fat person dies. I like it when people do nothing all over me. Men know things that are shifting all the time. A cat pukes up steam. Lukas is blind. Adam's disappeared.

Two-for-one shitbarn matricide. A slave to public humiliation. Testicle hatdance farmer is quaking. The ex-president gets shat on.

Break my face open, lazy inhabitor. That was the Whore's instruction to Adam. Adam broke a chair over her pussy. A blonde person sat down on it.

Simon eats Ned's dick cheese. Summertime gayness is so refined. I'm eating the medicinal warbler tonight. The Pope's asshole won't remain a virgin.

Franny was stuck in a loveless marriage. She decided to go to the other america and do something about it—and right away. She immediately pounced on Adam's erected sausage. Boy did she grind that sausage with an extreme movement of her pelvic area. Oh it was so fine, she just had to drink some wine. She put it in her ass and smelled just like a therapist!

Samuel fucked the hog's shadow.

Slap me in the face before you fuck me, I wanna know I'm alive for you. Fat fuck parrot flies into the ass of god, brings back justice to the human race. A goddamn flea concert is held in honor of the lost maggot up Lukas's buttcrack; please, bring us over another stick of butter to melt over the shiftless ones. Teenage terrorist with gasmask on pisses on Adam's face. Jack eats Lukas's foot and barebacks him at the same time. The drugged savior got his ass rimmed for christmas.

Twink with a boner on rollerskates eating strawberry cheese-cake cupcake skated right into the Whore's vaginal opening. Jesus Christ just had a baby on my fears. Peter shaved his best friend's tacit muslim balls with a rusty razor. He believed in his country.

God showed the Whore what her mouth was made to be used for. The martian cum guzzler has no hair. The martian's tits fell off into the blender. We had blue milk for dinner that evening.

I love it when you orient me towards your broken snatch. The disused bottle just found a new foundation. It's called the anus of your mother's corpse.

What's new in the world is I just found out. Ninja twat comma does a backflip against the column. A spider's entropy is morbid. No more fuckers to have a hot dog heart attack. He put Susanne's head through the bass drum as he fucked the shit out of her unlubricated asshole. The Whore picks wild flowers.

The midget screams as his butthole falls right out of his nose. Lukas knocks all of Taylor's teeth out, one by one by three, with the heel of his sneaker. That way the teeth won't get in his way when he's cockgagging the poor lad. I got cockblocked by an alien. No one who has any hair is worth speaking to.

Lukas shaved all of his armpit hair off and put it in Samuel's oatmeal. Samuel the fuckface fucked well. His eyes would never go to hell. He had seen things, but the Pope had blessed them. He gave his eyeballs to Adam so that Adam could complete his suicide mission with vision fission. I have no oracular heartache. The tits of god squirt sour milk on to the faces of the orgymakers. Zach smoked ten cigarettes and went away to his mother.

Squirt vaseline from a tube into a baby's open mouth, then shove your fist down into its innards and sing hallelujah. Ponytail squirrel crawls into open crevice of whore's split knee, buries its ego in there. Cannibalize your grandmother's cunt as a father's day present. The wrath of syntheticism pulls you into the graveyard for a fight.

Now Arnold just pulled a hamstring muscle fucking Adam's elastic bunghole as Adam's fist goes down Lukas's throat; with his other hand, he jacks off Zach's trunklike member, as Peter and Taylor each fuck one of his eyesockets, while the Whore and Matthew fuck each of his nostrils, and Marc gives him a blowjob.

Where is Murphy.

The soviet nun has so much hair. Something that's dead that lives on each of us. It keeps growing and growing. She is really upset about it, and she goes to the barber and demands it all be cut off. The barber is in a wheelchair; he doesn't know how to cut anyone's hair. And so she has to take the scissors and do it herself. She cuts every last one of those crippled midget's hairs right off, then flushes them down the toilet where they get to drown in all that delightful sewage. Matthew.

A jaguar's anal leakage just set off the fire alarm. Three amoeba are involved in a pretty heavy daisychain operation. I wanna fill yr ego with salami and eat it. Lukas has bad breath. Tim's cock just hit the floor. He was reduced to the status of a name.

Fannie Mae rubs her vagina across the floor. She's wearing pig ears and nothing else. Adam comes up and pisses on her face. She squeals with delight as she slashes her left tit wide open with a boy scout knife.

A fat cunt named Jupiter came over to see me. She had a cat o' nine tails sticking out of her hairstyle. She wanted to eat a muffin, and so I let her.

The cat gave the dog a blowjob in the pink-walled room. Next to them, Adam fucked Matthew. Arnold rode Taylor home like it was Saturday night at the rodeo. Zach ate a parrot. Peter burned the house down and yelled at himself for crying.

A woman named Wendy has no moles on her body. She is free.

Susan sucks my balls. I put the barrel of a gun in her mouth and she sucks that too.

Arnold fucked a french fry. Normal sensation wasn't good enough for him; he had to have it all. In this sense, he was just like all the others. All the others were just like Arnold. Arnold had no business being there.

Lukas licked out Adam's crevice. Adam's empty eyesockets filled with jizz. Zach was in the women's room, licking out all the toilet bowls he could gain access to. The sound of breaking glass. Matthew and Peter puked cum on Nathan's salad. The hairs of a teenage armpit. Arnold makes some corn on the cob.

It's gonna taste so yum, I can't wait to eat it! Matthew takes a polaroid of Adam's rosebud.

[...]

After we had done our respective business on each other, we got into the bomb truck. Police stopped us. Police is gonna die.

CHAPTER 25

The national forest.
In which
they find
their animals.

The Suiciders were on the run again, like lobsters down an empty shore. I'm so glad we could come here in this luxury vehicle, Adam, would you have eyes to see. Fast food children are so restless in the woodlessness. That was before we arrived at the hallucination. The word *over* in capital letters.

Police is after us. It wants to mold us into a shape that's not natural to our collective temperament. Rolling on down the vehicle is vague. The highway is such a sexual animal, I need it to roll over me.

Adam drove the car. He didn't need eyes; he had his parrot to tell him where to go. Zach sat in the backseat slowly drifting. He had a dream about Lukas. Hey guys, Lukas just came to me, I think I know where he is. But nobody was listening. Adam's eyelessness.

Peter was in the backseat crying. He wrote a letter to his mother. Someone was about to whip him, and he wanted to know if Arnold minded. Arnold's such an interesting person. Too bad he is with us on our journey. No one could sing.

Rather. Thin metallic hairs sprouted from Zach's skull. The Whore came and combed them. Are there any whims left you have for me to satisfy. No, he said. We dismissed her.

The Whore went off down the highway sunset to play with her drill.

Car stalled in the middle of the enterprise. Matthew stepped out and cursed. Taylor wanted to leave us. He was so frustrated by the way the journey had turned out. Give me my money back, you horseturd. Taylor stabbed his own mother in the breast. That's why he was on the run from the law. Police doesn't know what he looks like anyway.

The skin nearly burned off of Matthew's hands in his process of trying to fix the car. He wanted to hold himself silent, but he wasn't quite skinless enough to feel glad. The wind made a new canoe out of our static. Adam did you just stab the transmission. Get your attitude silence out of the thin canister. Don't worry, the soup is organic, and so is your mother.

Longevity's delusion had soon been slashed, a tire in the parking lot of someone else's fast food. Dildo dogfarm had its detractors. Adam parked the car on the side of the highway and ran outside, his head spinning through the airwaves, his tongue lolling out so that he could taste the sensation of a nation away from here. Satan's eating dogfood. That's what Peter says.

The rest of the happenstance couldn't matter. Police is after us now. We couldn't be pressed too hard, or else a toolbox would pop out. I'll have the drunken sailor platter. A thin herb drew notice to its own awareness. Matthew smoked a lollipop.

Peter's in the backseat crying. Taylor tries to comfort him. We've already tasted all the flavors, Arnold. Can't you see where we're going? Neither can I? At least I know something. That's impossible. The only true knowledge there is, it's all been evaded successfully throughout. A woman gets kissed by Christ. She is in the parking lot singing. The way this americana has gone, I don't know how she could afford herself.

Get out of the bomb truck Matthew it needs more fertilizer for an instant.

A pleathery Saturday. Politics took a dump on my lawn mower. Velvet priest comes over to inoculate us against rainburn. The child stood over the river, imagining. No sooner had he done that, then he had to stop. He went in the way of change. A bright new future tapdanced across the lonesome horizon. No new clichés could get born yet. It was too early in the century to determine which of them would matter least, in the parallel longevity of the de-tuned multiverse.

Marc editorialized all over Matthew's sphincter. Marc, we must say, had been born of Matthew. That is why the two of them knew so much about the other; they were alike. If there is one thing you can count upon before the bombs arrive, it is that the swallows have televisions strapped to their pelvises. Ave maria, my sweetheart. Hey Peter give me five dollars.

I liked it in the old way better. Is it really silver in your hair? Swing from the other vine. Adam has a thing against paying for happiness.

They kept trying to find Lukas, but eventually, they had had to give it all up and leave the basement. Your artful metal thermometer poses a horniness I am unwilling to reciprocate. Nasty birds without wings float on up to the ceiling. Pretend to like anything I'm up against. The ceiling is stacked pretty large also.

There was a pretty good shithouse for teenagers back in the mustang. Nobody went out to ride me yet. Guess they couldn't get enough screwlords to manage. A monster was on fire that night. The FBI lard pile Adam wanted to visit. Can't you assist me in this derangement? I was happier the day I got sat on. I'm on the negative machinery right now; we see the yellow arrows pointing backwards, and so naturally we will go the other way. The electricity that almost happens when you're riding down the highway.

One forecast at a time, please! Zach shouted at the cats out the window as we sped on past. It felt so good to be moving again finally, after all that time cooped up hiding from the big fat law. We only killed as many polices as we had to. They had unleashed their eagles on us, was the problem. Now we had to escape both the police eagles and the Goddamn (i.e. White Nothing, Zach's new name for it). There was a lively ass party going on in the trunk, however, where Arnold and Peter had insisted on being locked up. It was their favorite part of the bomb truck, you see, the one place where they could see each other through all the darkness.

A teenager's testicles were among us. Anyone with long black hairs whose name happens to be Lukas is advised to contact us immediately. A purple violence has much heat. We're talking to the firemen right now. Reststop hookers don't wanna go for a ride. The satisfied lobster crawls down the side of Zach's fake head.

That jazz music makes me throw up, Peter said to Adam in the front seat. Change it right away. Taylor yelled for everyone to be quiet. He said he felt a new prayer coming on. Will you lead us in it then, doofus, or are you merely here to shatter the membrane. The manager poured Adam's breakfast down the drain. Get out of my fast food now before the law's phone number gets exploited. C'mon, Adam, we don't need his tear-stained porridge. But I want a piece of my identity back. You lost that in the second chapter.

Zach hung Lukas's electric guitar up over the gas station flagpole. We drove away and watched the wind play a powerchord.

We were led by something most teenagers couldn't enumerate. Our path was togetherness to be ahead of the limestalked whereworth. So many of us had toes and personal problems to deal with. I am feeling nostalgic for my early death. Farting llama got attacked at the zoo.

Whatever happened to Adam the percussionist, tomorrow's india children will sing.

Some thought of us as a continent that year-and-a-half; but really, we were a decade. A youthful hangover that lasted much past its pubitive primal. Stern in the ocean we once thought of creating, until steam evaporated most of our higher ambitions. A socket worn oppositional can't fill the absent lava spewing forth our lastic greenery. To drive the bomb truck, we needed to afford the dynamic fabrics our absent fathers' life work could de-attain.

Fissuring through the stream of another america's highway system, we bid adieu to the figure of the eternal mother, who greatly regretted her absenting herself from the conclusionary mission (the missionary conclusion). Armed professionals have to have their rivals, otherwise they will never be paid. A whale's toilet is the same atomic ocean he swims in, after all.

Here comes something funny to laugh about for a real long time you guys. My mother's shadow. A fat gay sasquatch neutering job found out its transmission limitations. The holy panda. Bombs barded. The fur. I want my former father married to another man? Adam and Peter held hands. They wanted to get us through the day. They volunteered to be arrested.

Oh shit the perennial taco. I don't really blame you for not liking me. I voted for myself president too in the last election. We all did. Just admit it to yourself before you go on flaming. A choice is screaming.

I wanna get to know you the way you satisfy. Says Adam. He is talking to no one, the passengerside window. These socks are itching my feet. So take them off, you dingbat! I don't want to journey to the other world without them. There are no virgins there. That I can come to understand. If only there were enough time…

The hysteria is what my androgyny was once about. Then youth passed, a shotgun up my dollish crevice. A prime maximalization to hold the truth gun! Reality boys are savoring this gay barn. People are strangled just trying to subsist on what they provoke. That havoc doesn't belong to you; put it down. Now.

It's undesigned, the resignation service. Who your friends would be? Fellated by the code. I don't really believe in people who are true to their roots. The cat just sat in the armchair circle and cried. Once you hang your dick out of my pocket, I'll send you a friendly reminder.

The chase was chasing them down. Then they all got stopped, when a cascade of robots had blocked the highway to sing christmas carols to the daily commuters. Adam just shat all over Peter's imagination. The bomb truck busted through the wall of robots in order to keep the chase alive. We need to find a brand new forest to violate. This can't continue the way our armpits have let us be this alive. Sludge is the only reason.

I don't like what the wind's doing when you look at me like that. Change it, and fast.

Peter said I wanna change my name to Martha before I die. Adam says you're not allowed to. But Zach's the one who makes the rules around here. Zach's mouth has temporarily fallen off.

Taylor has an armpit. Are you ready to die, Taylor? Taylor just giggles to himself whenever anyone mentions the word *die*. He thinks it's just so lovely to affirm the negative. In the worst case disaster scenario, his mother always sounded her vulva alarm. His autobiography rang hollow that august spring afternoon.

Reality is glum, Peter says to Arnold. Arnold is not really okay to answer.

Oh the drugless finite is too tight. Antipathy's much like a disaster. You really can't be this authoritative when you're waving. Zach's fairness makes him sick at times. He won't let other people hyphenate his existence. That's too bad, when you're eating a salad legacy. Tinny fatwas are like sharks that have a direction.

I don't know why you're saying something, it must hurt you. Trashed vestibule is annihilated neatly. Once they had managed to escape Police's metal detector of idiocy, they had their own to confront. Lucky freedom! This is an owl's dichotomy. This gesture such a lonely feral. Singularity's cockring.

Oh, that evil gyration is thin. Have you been to the doctor yet? You must know whether you are in the proper physical condition for suicide. It is important not to take any risks; you could ruin things for the others. We would be so grateful. The aspiring is what keeps us grounded. I think of ruins more often than saturday.

Here we go falling off the foreigner it's so annoying. What we've been conditioned to save is not our feeling. The thumb is in the livestock.

A happy bird get away from here. We are always always on the highway. This insistence is much heeded, a self-inflicted gunshot wound. An estonian prostitute oh much better. Those boys are unhappy again. You can't go chasing me down. Oh my enormous shitwanking legacy. Go into your savior, come back out again.

Life sure gets ugly when you're farting jealousy. Only so many of us turned our backs on the ruse. Mostly we were eager to find our Whore. We thank the black background for telling us. Screwed survivor isn't necessarily better; just watch the dolphins. It all makes sense from the second perspective. I appreciate your being so mediocre and loss of appetite. The fact-sharing police gets stabbed in the head. We scotchtaped his anatomy to our car windshield as a reminder and warning to other polices get the fuck out of our goddamn way.

Adam ran over a penguin on his way to the suicide forest. He was driving too fast, the White Nothing coming after us. The White Nothing has wings we can surely not benefit from. The mere tinge of sarcasm is such the sorrowful whale. We must admit these things to ourselves from time to time before linearity comes to defeat us. I want to go kung fu fighting. I want to see you erased. I want to see you here. You have such a pretty face. People are pissing on most saturnal enterprises these days. Here comes a position from the westerly outside to shock them all into bookcase realness.

Look, I just took a photo, are you listening to me now? A priest celebrates the demise of civilitory grenade-throwing. Chunky footfloggers try and invade this vehicle. We're not gonna let princess smart attack get busted before the rainbow expires. Hurry the fuck up Taylor and Adam, why can't the two of you drive this force thing as ones?

Here is that time to be a tiger (I'm flying). Purple anniversary to know the thing that Peter purports to be doing to Matthew in the backseat chickentime. Arnold is all sprawled out, already dying. We revivify him by blowing bubbles in his brain. Feed my hunger child? Which forest is this one now. No, that can't be right. We want the forest that precludes the most possibility.

It's okay the sun. Getting forested in the rain never deters the help from foaming. The latest constellation in the shape of Zach's misformed dong. Don't remember to smell the trophy please. I was happy to be with you that night you almost forgot to know that.

Just like it is dangerous to be a mouse, it is dangerous, oh, I forgot something. Are you lost in the shape of that house yet. Preternatural transfiber undemanding. It seems like you could almost be something. That was the night we put the sun on trial. The trail of silence had an open sore.

Oh shit, we just went past Lukas wearing a hat. Keep going. Don't let him see us, he might want to join.

Why don't we let him.

It's too late, the suicide mission's been closed down.

Only so many are meant to die this way.

We have to get inside to be defined.

We continued on down the romantic alleyway. I know exactly the spot in the forest that was haunted by skinned ghouls several years back, asserts Peter. Why the hell aren't you driving, then, fool? What is this a-team awareness plot without a blind leader, need I be. Zach snorts each time someone mentions an armpit ladder. Police is on fire anyway, you lard.

Police would never find us again. Neither could the White Nothing. We had brightly evaded. No notice can come unclean. We were sad to be aware, but that sadness would soon go elsewhere. The grand plot would always come clean whenever Taylor and Zach were on the putrid scene.

Come back here, Adam, I think we just found the right path to drive down.

Arnold's in the backseat shaving his stomach. The rest of us looked on, deeply uninterested. A glad thwacker, all my friends, and Matthew and Peter fade l'amour. Congressional nobodies: that was to be our enemy from here on out, now that most of our enemies were gone. There were none among us; finally we could go uncorroded.

It's been a long time since divinity chewed upon us, Zach announced solemnly. But Taylor here has done much to help us betray most of our former ambitions. Thank you, Taylor. On behalf of the enterprise, our situationality has been altered in the smoothest, stunningest way possible.

Taylor's so alarmed by the devotion, he doesn't know how to play it. So he just gathered leaves and sat with his legs behind his ears.

But I'm getting ahead of myself, as always. We weren't even there yet. Peter had taken the wrong path, so Adam elbowed him in the liver, said move over, let me drive you imbecile. Peter protested, but then Zach said no let him, we need a blind navigator to right all of the goddamn wrongs this roguester has just put upon us.

We drove into the national forest at nighttime. We all disappeared in the woods, silently, agreeing to meet back at the bomb truck in an hour. Our teen suicide pact was real and our lives would be beginning soon. We arrived back at the truck at midnight. Arnold had found a monkey. Marc had a squirrel. I got a baby cub. Adam had an anteater. Zach had a squid. Peter had a ferret. We sat in the truck with the bombs strapped to our backs and our animals in our laps and awaited the detonation.

About the Author

Travis Jeppesen is the author of two novels, *Victims* and *Wolf at the Door*. His writings on art and film regularly appear in *Artforum*, *Art in America*, and *Whitehot Magazine of Contemporary Art*. He lives in Berlin and London, where he teaches at the Royal College of Art.